W9-BPM-672

She felt for him—

a sudden empathy that startled and disturbed her. Laura didn't want to feel for anyone but her daughter. She had far too much responsibility in her life right now to leave room for a handsome firefighter.

Luckily he didn't seem to expect an answer from her. Ryan touched her arm lightly, and she felt the warmth of that touch right through the fabric of her sweater.

"Hey, I'll work out my problems. But thanks for listening. I'll be glad to return the favor anytime."

She managed to smile, to nod. Ryan meant well, but she didn't have any intention of sharing her inner thoughts with anyone, least of all him. He'd come too far into her life already.

MARTA PERRY

has written everything from Sunday school curriculum to travel articles to magazine stories in twenty years of writing, but she feels she's found her home in the stories she writes for Love Inspired.

Marta lives in rural Pennsylvania, but she and her husband spend part of each year at their second home in South Carolina. When she's not writing, she's probably visiting her children and her beautiful grandchildren, traveling or relaxing with a good book.

Marta loves hearing from readers and she'll write back with a signed bookplate or bookmark. Write to her c/o Steeple Hill Books, 233 Broadway, Suite 1001, New York, NY 10279, e-mail her at marta@martaperry.com or visit her on the Web at www.martaperry.com.

HER ONLY HERO

MARTA PERRY

Steeple
Hill®

Published by Steeple Hill Books™

If you purchased this book without a cover you should be aware
that this book is stolen property. It was reported as "unsold and
destroyed" to the publisher, and neither the author nor the
publisher has received any payment for this "stripped book."

STEEPLE HILL BOOKS

Steeple
Hill®

ISBN 0-373-87323-9

HER ONLY HERO

Copyright © 2005 by Martha Johnson

All rights reserved. Except for use in any review, the reproduction
or utilization of this work in whole or in part in any form by any
electronic, mechanical or other means, now known or hereafter
invented, including xerography, photocopying and recording, or in
any information storage or retrieval system, is forbidden without
the written permission of the editorial office, Steeple Hill Books,
233 Broadway, New York, NY 10279 U.S.A.

All characters in this book have no existence outside the imagination of
the author and have no relation whatsoever to anyone bearing the same
name or names. They are not even distantly inspired by any individual
known or unknown to the author, and all incidents are pure invention.

This edition published by arrangement with Steeple Hill Books.

® and TM are trademarks of Steeple Hill Books, used under license.
Trademarks indicated with ® are registered in the United States Patent
and Trademark Office, the Canadian Trade Marks Office and in other
countries.

www.SteepleHill.com

Printed in U.S.A.

Help carry one another's burdens,
and in this way you will obey the law of Christ.
—Galatians 6:2

This story is dedicated to Gary and Arddy Johnson, with much love. And, as always, to Brian.

Chapter One

"I suppose you'd better come in."

Laura McKay had a feeling that sounded ungracious. She tried to make amends by forcing a smile as she stood back to let the uniformed firefighter step into the foyer of her brick townhouse.

The man glanced through the archway to the bare, dusty area she hoped would eventually be a ground-floor shop. Searching for something to find unsafe, no doubt.

"Sorry to bother you." He consulted the clipboard he carried. "Ms. McKay, is it? I'm Ryan Flanagan, from the Suffolk Fire Department."

He didn't recognize her, then. Funny, because she'd known Ryan Flanagan from the moment she opened the door.

Ryan hadn't changed all that much from the tall, handsome football hero he'd been in high school. One of the popular Flanagan brothers, with those deep-blue eyes and that cleft in his strong chin, he'd had every girl at Suffolk High School longing to be the recipient of one of his teasing smiles, including her.

Well, that was a long time ago. It didn't matter that he hadn't remembered the shy underclassman who had admired him from afar.

"I don't understand why you're here." She glanced up the stairs of the three-story townhouse, longing to get back to the work she'd set herself for the day. "I have all the necessary permits for the renovation, and the building has already been inspected by your department."

He shrugged, smiling. The smile was, unfortunately, just as devastating as it had been in high school.

"Just one of those necessary things, I'm afraid. Someone called the department with a complaint, so we're obligated to check it out."

"Someone complained about me?" That jerked her mind away from the wallpaper she'd been removing. "Who?"

"Anonymous." He shrugged again. "It happens. If you'll just let me take a walk-through and check things out, I'll get out of your hair."

He glanced at her head as he spoke, and she put up her hand to discover that the bandanna she'd tied on to protect her wiry mane was thoroughly covered with plaster dust. She swatted at it uselessly and then pulled the thing off. What difference did it make what she looked like, anyway? The important thing was to get back to work.

Her nerves tightened in a way that had become too

familiar lately. Time was running out, and she had to finish the job. If she didn't—

Well, *if* didn't bear thinking about.

So the sooner she got rid of Ryan Flanagan the better. She waved a hand toward the staircase. "We might as well begin at the top. That's where I've been working today."

She started up the wooden stairwell, not touching the gritty railing. The wood was mahogany under all that dirt, and eventually it would shine. The whole place would.

His footsteps sounded behind her. "You're actually rehabbing this place yourself?"

"What's wrong with that?" She sounded tart, she supposed, but she'd heard that incredulous tone from enough people since she'd started this job.

"Nothing, I guess. But this place has been deteriorating for so long I figured eventually it would be torn down. Or fall down."

Laura touched the intricate molding she'd uncovered when she'd renovated the second-floor landing. She loved the smooth, aged feel of it under her fingers, loved knowing she'd uncovered its beauty.

"You'd be surprised. The place has been standing since 1810, and they built to last then."

The three-story brick townhouse on the edge of Suffolk's historic district might look decrepit, but she wasn't giving up on it. It had the potential to be a showpiece. Besides, it was all she and her daughter had between them and an uncertain future.

She glanced toward the apartment door as they

passed it. She'd fixed the apartment up first, so she and Mandy would have a decent place to live. Mandy was occupied right now with a new coloring book, and she wouldn't hear them.

Her heart cramped. No, Mandy wouldn't hear them.

They emerged into the open space at the top of the stairs. Ryan looked around doubtfully, and she understood what he was seeing.

The top floor looked like a barren, dusty wreck. Shreds of faded floral wallpaper clung to old horsehair plaster, which had crumbled away to the underlying lath in places. The May sunshine filtering through high, cracked windows, lit up every flaw.

Ryan touched a dangling strip of wallpaper. "You think you can actually make something livable of this?"

She wasn't used to explaining herself to people, but Ryan, with his uniform and that report sheet on his clipboard, wasn't just anyone. That insignia he wore gave him the right to probe. Tension skittered along her nerves. He could shut her down.

"Yes, I do. Believe it or not, I have a degree in interior design."

His dark eyebrows lifted. "This isn't interior design. It's construction. Or maybe demolition."

"My father was a contractor," she said quickly. "I learned from the best."

He nodded, still looking doubtful, and started around the third floor. Holding her breath, she followed him. She ran a clean work site—her father had always insisted on that. He wouldn't find any junk around to complain about.

Ryan's attention to his inspection gave her ample time to take a look at the man he'd become. The seriousness with which he seemed to take his job was new. The Ryan she remembered had never taken anything seriously, but he'd always seemed able to charm his way out of the trouble his recklessness had gotten him into.

She wasn't surprised by the neat blue uniform with the Suffolk Fire Department patch that fit his tall figure so well. All the Flanagans had been wedded to the fire department. There'd never been much doubt as to what Ryan would do with his life.

He turned toward her as they reached the stairwell again, smiling. She had to fight not to respond too warmly to that smile. Ryan had added some breadth and height since high school, and the sense of maturity combined with his uniform made a powerful package.

"Looks like you've got everything under control up here. Shall we check out the rest?"

She could breathe again. She nodded and started down the stairs, feeling him behind her.

"My apartment on the second floor is completely finished and we're moved in. It's not necessary for you to go through that, is it?" She paused, looking up at him.

"I don't think—" His gaze fixed on something over her shoulder, interrupting the words.

She turned. Mandy stood there, hand on the doorknob, looking at them with a grave, questioning expression in her dark-brown eyes.

Laura reached her in a few steps and touched her daughter's curly brown hair. "It's okay," she said, signing as she did so. "I'm showing the fireman around. There's nothing to worry about."

She looked toward Ryan. If she saw pity in his eyes, she'd let him know what she thought about that.

But Ryan was squatting to a five-year-old's level, and she read only friendliness in his face.

"Hi. My name's Ryan." He finger-spelled the name carefully. "What's yours?"

He spoke naturally, apparently copying what she'd done, and she appreciated that. With her two hearing aids, Mandy might be picking up something.

"My daughter's name is Mandy." She continued to sign as she spoke. Mandy should never feel left out. "You know sign language."

"You don't need to sound quite so surprised." He grinned. "Firefighters need to be able to communicate with people we run into on the job. Unfortunately you've seen almost my whole vocabulary."

Ryan seemed to have turned into a responsible member of society. Maybe she should stop thinking of him as the reckless, laughing kid he'd been in high school.

She gave Mandy a little push toward the apartment. "You finish your picture. We'll probably be done by then."

Ryan waved to her. "Bye, Mandy."

When the door closed behind her, the smile slid from his lips. "She's a beautiful little girl. Has she been deaf since birth?"

"Yes." She started down the steps, hoping he'd take the hint. Her personal life was off limits.

"Her father?"

Apparently Ryan wasn't good at taking hints.

"My husband died a year ago."

"I'm sorry." He stopped next to her at the bottom of the stairs, and she was aware of how tall and solid he was. "It must be rough, trying to handle everything on your own."

Her smile felt frozen. "Not at all. At least, not if we can finish this up so I can get back to work."

He should have taken offense at that, but he just studied her for a moment, his deep-blue eyes intent but friendly. Then he nodded.

"Okay. Let's take a quick look around the downstairs."

"Fine."

She followed him through the downstairs living room, mentally chastising herself. He'd just been expressing sympathy. She had to stop being so sensitive about her independence.

They pushed through the swinging door to the old kitchen, and she wrinkled her nose. She'd done nothing here yet, and the cracked linoleum and rusted sink rebuked her.

They reached the back door without speaking. Ryan pulled the door open, stepped onto the back porch, and frowned at the stack of wood and construction rubbish piled against the wall.

"I know," she said quickly. "It shouldn't be there."

"It's a hazard." His tone was uncompromising.

"I ordered a Dumpster last week. I don't know why

they haven't brought it yet." It was yet another of a long string of things that had gone wrong recently.

"Do you want me to call them? They might move a little faster at a request from the fire department."

"No."

He was just being nice, she reminded herself. She didn't need to bite his head off.

"I'll take care of it," she added more evenly. "They promised me it would be here days ago."

He nodded, scribbling something on a sheet and then handing it to her. "This just confirms that we've spoken about it. If the situation isn't remedied in a few days, we'll have to cite you."

"Don't worry." Her lips were stiff. "It will be."

He studied her for a moment and then gave her that slightly lopsided smile she'd once yearned to see. "Don't look so worried. This is just a formality. I'm sure you'll take care of the problem."

She forced a return smile. "Thanks."

He stepped off the porch. "My name and number are on the form. If you'd like me to get after the trash company, just give me a call."

"I can manage."

She could do whatever she had to do, despite the addition of Ryan Flanagan to the list of factors complicating her life since she'd taken on this project.

Her daughter's future depended on her success with the building. She couldn't count on anyone else for help—not her family, not her in-laws, not God.

A fierce wave of maternal love swept through her. That didn't matter. For Mandy, she could do anything.

* * *

Ryan piled into the truck behind his older brother, Seth, heart pounding as it always did at the shrilling of the alarm. He glanced at his watch. Six-thirty. Fire could have caught people asleep at this hour of the morning.

Seth, taking his new rank of lieutenant very seriously, was listening to the info coming in on his radio.

"Three-fourteen Delaware Street. Isn't that the place you inspected yesterday?"

"Yes." Ryan's nerves clenched. "Woman and a child in residence. A deaf child."

He hadn't gotten their images out of his mind yet. Laura McKay, with that mop of wiry dark hair springing out around her grave, determined face. Her daughter, Mandy—brown curls, her mother's dark eyes, and those two hearing aids in her small ears.

"What did you find wrong?"

"Trash on the back porch that should have been in a Dumpster. That's it."

He should have called the company about that, even though Laura McKay had told him not to.

"That meshes with what the caller said—a blaze on the back porch." The siren wailed as they took the corner. "We'll attack from the alley. You and Dave can do the entry."

He nodded. Seth was giving him the rescue. Nice to know his big brother had that much faith in him, even though their new relationship of lieutenant to firefighter sometimes rubbed both of them the wrong way.

Of course, if the posting to the arson squad he'd applied for came through, it would eliminate the problem. He'd have a different boss, a different job. He hadn't told anyone about it yet, not sure himself how he felt about the change.

He pushed the whole business from his mind. There wasn't room to think about anything else when he went into a fire scene.

They shrieked up the alley, the backs of the buildings a little seedy here compared to the polish of the historic district in the next block. Seth leaned forward, probably assessing what they had to deal with.

Seth's caution was a good quality for a lieutenant. All Ryan wanted to do was get in there and make the grab. His body itched with the need to move.

A bystander in robe and slippers rushed up to the apparatus. "I'm the one called it in. There's a woman and kid live there—they didn't come out."

Ryan pulled out his hand ax as his feet hit the ground. Dave Hanratty was right behind him, both of them fully geared up with masks. Flames licked at the wooden porch, but the building's brick walls would slow the blaze down.

He nodded to Dave and together they charged toward the door. A couple of quick hits, a kick, and they were in.

Smoke billowed through the downstairs, and a smoke alarm wailed relentlessly. If Laura heard it, why hadn't she gotten out by now?

"Stairs." He pointed with the ax. "Apartment on the second floor."

They hit the steps running, their footsteps thundering on the wooden treads. No flames had reached this area, but the smoke was the danger. Smoke could kill.

He reached the second-floor landing a step ahead of Dave and raised his ax. Before he could swing, the door opened.

Laura stumbled toward them. The little girl in her arms was partially covered with a blanket, but her small face was pinched with terror.

He reached for the child. The woman tried to hang on to her.

"I'll take her—" Her words died in a fit of coughing.

He grabbed the little girl, ignoring her frightened wail and the mother's protests. This was no time for politeness. He passed the child to Dave, who started back down the steps with her.

He grabbed Laura's arm. "Is there anyone else in the building?"

"No." She tried to pull away from him. "You scared Mandy. I could have carried her out."

When it came to stubborn, this woman took the cake. He yanked her to the stairs. "Tell me about it later. Right now we're getting out."

Luckily she'd shoved her feet into shoes, so he didn't have to worry about her getting cut up. He hustled her down the steps. The front door stood open now, and together they rushed out into the fresh morning air.

The paramedic unit had already pulled up to the curb, and the crew from the secondary tank truck was wetting down the adjoining buildings.

He took Laura straight to the paramedics—his sister Terry's team, thank goodness. Terry was the best. She was already checking out the little girl.

Mandy struggled to get away from Terry's hands, reaching toward her mother. Laura dropped to her knees on the wet pavement, coughing, and swept her child into her arms.

The lump in his throat might have been from the smoke, but he didn't think so.

Thank You, Father.

He suspected Dave was saying the same prayer. Any day they got people out safely was a good day.

"You need to let us check you out." Terry's voice was gentle but authoritative as she peeled the little girl away from her mother.

Laura nodded, but Mandy took one look at him and began to wail again.

Quickly he stripped off the mask and helmet and squatted next to her. "Hey, Mandy, it's me." He pulled off his gloves so he could sign his name. "Ryan."

The wailing stopped and the child's dark eyes widened, some of the fear leaving them.

"This is just my mask." He had to gesture to make up for the signs he didn't know. "See, Terry is going to give you one, too."

Mandy clutched her mother's hand, but she let Terry fit the oxygen mask on her face.

Terry glanced up. "Thanks, Ry. We're going to take them both to the hospital."

"I'm all right—" Laura began, but the words were interrupted by a fit of coughing.

"Just to check you out," Terry said gently. "Don't worry."

"Listen to my sister." He gave Laura a reassuring smile. "Trust me, she knows best."

She nodded, clasping the little girl close as he and Terry helped them into the rig. "Thank you," she murmured, and the door closed.

He watched the unit out of sight. They'd be all right. He and Dave had gotten to them in time.

He turned back to the building. A sense of relief went through him. Thanks to their fast response, the crew nearly had the blaze out already. By the looks of things, the damage probably wasn't going to be severe.

Still, thinking about the job Laura was trying to do, he felt a pang of sympathy. She'd already had her hands full. Now, it looked as if her life had just gotten a whole lot tougher.

Laura trudged up the stairs to the second-floor apartment, following the yellow beam of her flashlight in the darkness. The staircase looked like Mount Everest at the moment. Apparently the doctors had been right about the effects of smoke inhalation.

I'm fine. That's what she'd kept repeating to the doctors all day so they'd let her go.

Mandy was spending the night at the hospital. *Just to be on the safe side,* they'd said. She'd stayed there, too, until her daughter fell asleep. She'd been tempted to go to sleep herself in the vinyl chair next to Mandy's bed.

But she kept thinking about the building. How bad was it? She'd been told the fire department had doused the flames quickly, but no one had told her how severe the damage was. She hadn't been able to sleep for thinking about it. Finally she'd known she had to see for herself.

So she'd come. She'd change her clothes and get Mandy's favorite teddy bear to take back to the hospital, just in case her daughter wakened in the night. And she'd check out the damage to the only asset they had to their names.

Then she could go back to the hospital and try to sleep in that chair, once she knew the worst.

She pushed herself up the last few steps, feeling as if she carried an enormous weight on her shoulders. The apartment door was closed, but not locked. Had she closed it in the flurry of getting out, when Ryan had manhandled her down those stairs? She didn't remember.

Inside, she swung the light around, half afraid of what she'd see. Her breath came out in a sigh of relief. The apartment was untouched. The acrid scent of smoke still hung in the air, but that was minor in comparison to what she'd been imagining.

Coughing a little, she crossed to the closest window and opened it a few inches at the top. Cool night air rushed in, fanning her face. She'd deal with airing out the rest of the apartment later.

She went through into the bedroom. The closet door was closed, and she pulled it open. Not too bad. The closed door had protected her clothing from the worst of the smoke.

She pulled out a pair of slacks and a shirt, changing quickly. She'd showered at the hospital, and a nurse had provided some cast-off clothing to replace the sooty, smoky pajamas she'd been wearing. She wouldn't be likely ever to wear those again.

A shudder ran through her. If the smoke alarm hadn't gone off, if someone hadn't seen the blaze and called the fire department, if—

No. She couldn't let herself keep reliving those terrifying moments when she'd struggled awake and run to Mandy's room. The problem would be to stop doing it.

She crossed the hall to her daughter's room, her stomach roiling. When she'd run in, terrified, Mandy had been awake, huddled under her quilt, clutching her teddy bear. Why hadn't she come to her mother when she realized something was wrong?

The bear, Teddy, lay abandoned on the rag rug next to the single bed. She scooped him up and held him close, feeling tears sting her eyes. We're all right. We're safe.

She wiped away the tears with the back of her hand. She had no time for crying. The clock was ticking.

In three weeks her prospective buyer would be here to check out the building. The specialist could call at any time to schedule Mandy's cochlear implant. The two most important things in her life sped toward her.

She had to be ready. She suppressed a flicker of panic.

Okay. Carrying the bear, she started back downstairs. She'd take a quick look at the damage and then head back to the hospital. And tomorrow—

She frowned, swinging the beam of light around the front room of the downstairs. Water from the fire hoses hadn't mixed very well with the dirt. Would she be able to bring Mandy back here tomorrow? Maybe, if the power company restored the electricity.

If not, that would mean a motel, and how she'd pay for that, she couldn't imagine. The panic flickered again and was beaten down. She could do this. She'd find a way.

Little as she wanted to, she had to check the back of the building, where the worst damage was. She picked her way carefully across the littered floor, feet moving in the yellow circle cast by the flashlight.

A loud thud sounded at the back of the house. Her heart stopped for an instant and then started thumping wildly. She heard a scuffling sound, then the rumble of a masculine voice, followed by several loud bangs.

The sensible thing was to run out and call the police. She wasn't feeling very sensible. Instead, rage surged through her. It wasn't bad enough that she and her child had been forced out of their home by the fire. Now some lowlife was trying to get in and rob them. Well, he'd get more than he'd bargained for this time.

The flashlight beam touched a two-by-four about as long as a baseball bat. Perfect. She grabbed it and advanced on the door to the old kitchen.

Light gleamed from around the swinging door. Apparently her thief had come well-equipped.

Running on anger and adrenaline, she shoved the door open, raising her improvised weapon threateningly. A dark figure stood at the back door.

"What do you think you're doing? Get out of here!"

He swung around, and her breath caught. Ryan. Ryan Flanagan stood there, a hammer in one hand.

Chapter Two

Ryan lifted his hands. "I give up. Don't shoot."

Laura's heart pounded, as if once the adrenaline started to flow, she couldn't stop it. "I'm sorry." She realized she was still holding the two-by-four. It hit the ragged linoleum with a clatter.

He lowered his hands cautiously, probably not sure she was really disarmed. "I didn't mean to startle you. I thought you were at the hospital."

"I came back to check the house."

He nodded toward the teddy bear that was clutched under her arm. "And to find something important, I guess."

She held the bear a little tighter. "He's important to Mandy. She likes to sleep with him."

"How is she?" Ryan leaned against a sooty counter, hands braced against its edge, apparently not minding the dirt. He'd exchanged his uniform for jeans and a dark-blue knit shirt, and he'd picked up a streak of soot across the front of the shirt, presumably since he'd entered the house. The concentrated light of the torch cast his strong face into sharp relief.

She forced herself to concentrate, her wits still scattered after finding him here so unexpectedly. "She's going to be all right. The doctor thought she should stay until tomorrow to be sure there aren't any aftereffects from the smoke."

"That's good." He studied her face. "You look as if they should have kept you, too."

"I'm fine." She was getting tired of saying that. "I don't want to be rude, but what are you doing here?"

"Fixing the door." He gestured toward the door that led onto the porch, and she realized belatedly that the powerful torch he'd set on the counter was trained on the opening. The door sagged on its hinges.

"You don't have to do that."

He shrugged. "I broke it. Seems like the least I can do is fix it."

"I can take care of the door. I don't need any help." She had to sound strong, because she was unaccountably weepy at the thought that Ryan Flanagan had actually come back to do something for her.

"Not even from an old school friend?" He gave her the easy grin that charmed so readily.

She blinked, startled. "I thought you didn't recognize me."

"You're Laura Jane Phillips. At least, it used to be Phillips. You were a year behind me at Suffolk High. Am I right?"

She nodded. So he had remembered her. Or perhaps someone had told him who she was.

"Why didn't you tell me who you were yesterday?" His eyebrows lifted. "Or didn't you remember me?"

"No one could forget the Flanagans." She answered the second question first, evading his eyes. "I just—didn't think it was appropriate to get into old home week when you were here on business."

He leaned casually against the filthy counter, as if ready to stay and chat all night. "It bugged me all day, trying to figure out why you looked so familiar to me. How are your folks?"

"They've retired to Arizona. My dad's health isn't very good." The usual pang of concern gripped her heart at the thought of her father.

"I'm sorry to hear that. I guess otherwise he'd be here doing the renovation for you."

She nodded. It wasn't necessary to confide in Ryan that her father didn't know she was doing the rehab herself, for that very reason. If Dad knew, he'd try to come and probably kill himself in the process.

As for her mother—well, she'd stopped trying to figure her mother out a long time ago. She just knew she couldn't count on her for help with this or anything else.

Ryan relaxed his long frame against the counter, not seeming in any hurry to get on with the door-fixing. "Anyway, I didn't know you'd come back to Suffolk. I thought you were living in Philadelphia."

"How on earth would you know that?" She hadn't imagined he'd remember who she was, let alone know where she'd gone after school.

He grinned. "You're forgetting my mother, with her encyclopedic knowledge of anyone who's ever attended our church. Once I mentioned you, she trotted out everything she knew, including the fact that you were married and living in Philly. She was surprised we haven't seen you in church since you've been back."

Siobhan Flanagan had taught her in church school twice—once in kindergarten, then again in junior high. She had a gentle manner, a warm smile and a love that extended to even the most rebellious of teens.

Still, however warm her memories of Ryan's mother, she was not going to defend her failure to attend church to him. "Please greet her for me. And really, I can take care of the door."

He shoved away from the counter in a smooth, even movement. "Tell you what. You hold the boards and I'll pound. We'll have it secure in no time."

That was probably the fastest way to get him out of here, so she set the flashlight and teddy bear down and went to the door. The acrid scent of wet, burned wood from the back porch sent a wave of nausea through her, and she forced it down angrily.

Ryan had apparently brought a few two-by-fours with him, because the wood gleamed new. He put one of the boards against the door, and she braced it with both hands.

He used the hammer with quick, effective strokes. The board vibrated from his force, jolting her hands.

"So, after your husband's death, you decided to come home and buy this place." The pounding punctuated his words, and she felt the flex of his muscles where his arm brushed her shoulder.

"Not exactly. My husband had bought the building a couple of years ago for some business venture he had in mind, but he never got around to doing anything with it. So I decided to fix it up."

She wouldn't add that this building was the only legacy Jason had left her and Mandy. That everything else he'd received from his father had been frittered away on one foolish scheme or another, until his father had finally cut him off, saying Jason would have to pay for his own mistakes. Apparently he'd put her and Mandy in the mistake category.

"You plan to live here?" Ryan propped another board across the door, and it gleamed palely against the blackened frame.

"I'm fixing it up to sell. I have a buyer who has an option, if I can get the renovation done before she loses interest or finds something better."

Ryan paused, looking over his shoulder at her. Her pulse gave a little jump. Her hands were planted next to his on the board, and his face was only inches away.

"And then you'll leave Suffolk again?" He looked at her as if he really wanted to know. As if it might matter to someone what she did.

Her mouth was dry. From the smoke, she assured herself. Not because Ryan Flanagan had any effect on her.

She moistened her lips. "I haven't decided yet. Mandy is going to have a cochlear implant—at least I hope she is, if all the tests go well. I can't plan beyond that right now."

The implant could give Mandy a chance at a normal life. How could she think of anything else?

"At the hospital here?" His eyes lit with interest. "That'd be Dr. Marsh, I guess."

"You've heard of him." She was faintly surprised. Franklin Marsh was well-known to parents of deaf children, but why would Ryan know of him?

"My sister-in-law, Gabe's wife, trains animals to work with people who have disabilities. She introduced me to Dr. Marsh at a benefit. I understand he does good work."

"He's the best." She wouldn't trust her daughter's hearing and her future to anyone who wasn't. "If he decides Mandy will benefit from an implant, it will make all the difference in the world to us."

And if he did accept Mandy for the procedure, she somehow had to come up with the over fifty thousand dollars the process would cost. The minimal insurance program she was able to afford would cover Mandy's stay in the hospital, but it didn't cover a cochlear implant.

As if he felt all the things she didn't say, Ryan put his hand over hers where it rested on the board. "I hope it works out."

"Thank you." She cleared her throat. "I appreciate that. And really, I can finish up the door. I'm sure you have other things to do with your evening."

"I'm free as a bird." He pounded another nail in place. "And anyway, as far as I can see, it's finished."

He stood back, smiling at her. He was right. The door was secured.

He'd shaken off her protests and done exactly what he'd said he would. And he'd gotten more information from her than she'd confided in anyone in months.

She raised her eyebrows at him, dusting her hands off. "Do you always get your own way?"

His smile broadened into a grin. "If you remember my family, you ought to know that I grew up fighting a bunch of siblings to get what I wanted. I've had a lot of practice."

"I remember that you used to charm the teachers into letting you get away with murder."

Now why had she said that? The man would think she was flirting with him.

"Lies, spread by my brothers, no doubt." His smile assumed an angelic aspect. "I was always a serious student."

"Somehow I find that difficult to believe." And she also found it difficult to believe that she was standing here smiling at him, after everything that had happened this day.

"Why is it no one will take me seriously?" He dropped the hammer into a duffel bag and picked up the flashlight.

"Maybe because you don't take yourself seriously."

"Ouch, that hurt. A woman who sees right through me. I'd better watch out." He hefted the bag. "Anything else I can fix while I'm here?"

"Everything's fine." Well, it wasn't, but he ought to know what she meant. "I guess we'd better go out the front door, since you've nailed up the back."

He nodded, and then he unexpectedly clasped her hand in his. His face was very serious in the dim light. "I wish you and your daughter the best."

"Thank you."

Ryan's words had been the kind of simple statement anybody might make. They shouldn't make her throat go so tight.

She turned away quickly, feeling him behind her as she headed for the door to the living room. Ryan Flanagan had a way of slipping through her carefully prepared defenses as if they weren't even there.

So it was a good thing she wouldn't be seeing any more of him.

"Listen, Ryan, are you sure Laura McKay isn't going to mind our breaking into her house this way?"

Ryan's brother Gabe paused, leaning on the shovel he'd been using to scrape soot and crumbled plaster from the ground floor of Laura's building. Max, the yellow lab who was Gabe's seizure-alert dog, sniffed at a pile of rubble, tail waving.

"Why would she? We're only trying to help."

Ryan suspected Laura wouldn't see it that way, given her strong streak of independence. But no matter how much she might insist she didn't need help, she was wrong. By the time she got home from the hospital with Mandy, he hoped they'd have much of the fire clean-up done.

A handful of Flanagans had offered to come along today along with several other firefighters. His cousin Brendan had used his clout as pastor to round up some more volunteers from the congregation.

All told, probably twenty or thirty people hustled around Laura's property, sweeping, mopping, carting away fire rubbish. Now if he could just persuade Laura to accept the help they offered, everything would be fine.

Well, he'd cross that bridge when he got to it. He clapped his brother on the shoulder. "Come on, put your back into it. They'll be home from the hospital soon."

Gabe shrugged and went back to shoveling.

Their mother looked up from the broom she was wielding. "I'm sure Laura will be happy to see us." Siobhan Flanagan smiled. "And I'll be glad to see her. I remember her from church school, years ago. Laura was always such a sweet, shy little thing."

"She's changed since then, Mom."

"Well, of course people change. Being the single mother of a deaf child would make someone grow up in a hurry, I'd think. Poor child."

He wasn't sure whether her sympathy was for Laura or Mandy, but it didn't really matter. Mom had enough love to go around for any number of people.

If it came to pitting Laura's stubborn independence against his mother's determination to help, he wouldn't want to guess at a winner.

Even as he thought it, the front door swung open, letting in a shaft of May sunshine. Laura stood there, clasping Mandy protectively against her.

For a moment she didn't move. She just stood, looking around the room as if unable to believe what she was seeing. Then she turned toward him with what looked like an accusation in her dark eyes.

She probably intended to come straight for him, but his mother got to her first. "Laura, it's so good to see you." She swept Laura into a quick hug. "I'm Siobhan Flanagan. You remember me, don't you?"

"Mrs. Flanagan." Laura took a step back. "Yes, of course I do." She darted a glance toward Ryan. "You're Ryan's mother."

It sounded as if she wanted to follow that up with, *Why are you here?*

"We're helping with the clean-up." His mother wasn't deterred by any reserve on Laura's part. She waved toward the workers. "You remember Gabe, my oldest boy."

"Mom, I'm not a boy," Gabe protested automatically. He lifted his hand toward Laura. "Hi, Laura."

"And that's Brendan, my nephew. He's pastor of our church now, you know."

Laura nodded in Brendan's direction, not committing herself to any knowledge of his pastorship of Grace Church. "It's very nice of you to want to help out, but really, I can take care of this myself."

Ryan had warned his mother that Laura would respond that way, and he waited to see how she'd handle it.

She did it with a smile and a gentle touch on Mandy's hair. The little girl gave her a shy smile in return, and Laura put her down.

"You wouldn't turn us away when we're having so much fun, now would you? That wouldn't be kind."

Laura opened her mouth and closed it again. Clearly she didn't want to be accused of being unkind by turning away kindness from others. He tried to hide his expression.

"No, I—well, thank you."

She frowned at him, and he smiled blandly back. Maybe he ought to take lessons from his mother in how to approach someone as prickly as Laura was.

Nolie approached her. "Hi, I'm Nolie Flanagan. Gabe's wife." She bent toward Mandy, her hands signing fluently. "You must be Mandy."

Mandy nodded, giving her that shy smile.

"Would you like to go upstairs and help me make sandwiches for lunch?" She patted the rounded bulge of baby under her sky-blue top as she glanced at Laura. "Gabe is getting nervous about every little thing I do, but he agrees that making sandwiches won't hurt me."

"I don't know if Mandy will go with you," Laura began, and then stopped. Mandy was already putting her hand in Nolie's. "Well, I guess she will. Thank you."

She watched her daughter start up the steps with an expression that told Ryan clearly that she didn't want her daughter out of her sight. That caution was natural enough, he supposed, after what they'd been through, but Nolie would take good care of the child, and she'd be away from the mess and dirt.

When they'd disappeared toward the apartment, Laura swung around and headed straight toward him. She stopped a scant two feet away and scowled. "This is your doing, isn't it?" She kept her voice low, apparently not wanting everyone else to hear.

"Hey, I'm innocent."

She raised level dark brows. "Am I supposed to believe it's a total coincidence that my house is filled with Flanagans?"

"Some of them aren't. Flanagans, I mean. There are a couple of firefighters here, and some people from the church that Brendan recruited."

"Don't you mean *you* recruited?"

"Not me. All I did was mention the fire to my mother. She did the rest." He gave a mock shudder. "Trust me on this one. My mother may be soft-spoken, but you don't want to get between her and something she's decided to do."

"Do you really want me to believe you're afraid of your mother?"

He grinned. "You bet."

Well, not afraid of her, but concerned about her opinion. Maybe that was why he hadn't told his mother yet about applying to the arson squad.

"I don't believe you." She shook her head. "And anyway, that's not the point."

"Right. The point is that you want to do everything all by yourself."

He thought her lips twitched slightly. "Are you trying to make me sound like a two-year-old?"

"You said it, I didn't." Before she could respond, he raised both hands. "Let's declare a truce, okay? We're here. Is it really so hard to let us help you?"

"No. I'm just—"

"Super-independent. I figured that one out already. What I haven't figured out yet is why."

Her dark-brown eyes met his, and for an instant they held so much pain that it took his breath away. Then her usual shield dropped into place and she gave him a polite, meaningless smile.

"I guess all I can do is say thanks."

She turned away. He stood watching as she picked up a box and began loading debris into it.

Laura had her game face back on now. But he'd seen behind it, and that glimpse into her shook him. A man would have to be crazy to get involved with someone who was carrying that load of grief.

Not that he was even thinking about doing such a thing.

Laura was still wondering what she was doing when she arrived at the Flanagan house for dinner a few evenings later. She was usually quite good at getting out of things she didn't want to do. Unfortunately she'd found that Siobhan Flanagan was very difficult to keep saying no to.

Maybe it was because Siobhan had been her church-school teacher, back when she'd still had a child's faith, thinking that every problem could be solved by prayer. She was swept with a sudden wave of longing to be back in that church-school room, sitting in the child-size chair and hearing Bible stories told in Siobhan's soft, loving voice.

A person could never go back, although the Flanagans seemed to be doing a good job of keeping their lives just the way they'd been.

She held Mandy's hand as they started up the walk to the welcoming brick house. Everything about the neighborhood—the mature trees, the old-fashioned flowerbeds brimming with tulips and irises, the comfortable old two-story homes—said that here was a place where people found safety and serenity.

She smiled at her daughter as they reached the steps that led to the wide front porch. Pansies crowded pots on either side of the stairs, and a cushion-piled porch swing creaked a little in the breeze.

"Mrs. Flanagan has pretty flowers, doesn't she?"

Mandy nodded, her small face tense, and Laura's throat clenched. She was taking her daughter into the sort of situation she usually avoided, just because she couldn't say no to Siobhan.

"We don't have to stay long, okay? We can go home right after supper if you want to."

"Okay."

She smiled, touching Mandy's cheek. "Good talking, Mandy." Mandy didn't verbalize very often since her hearing had worsened, so it was an occasion for praise when she did.

She squeezed her daughter's hand, and together they approached the door. It was flung open before she could knock. Three children crowded around them, making Mandy shrink against her.

"They're here, they're here!" The oldest, a girl who must be about six or so, caught Mandy's hand and pulled her inside. "Grammy, they're here."

Flanagans. Obviously they were all three Flanagans, with the same reddish-gold hair and blue eyes. If only they weren't quite so friendly—it was like being surrounded by a bunch of puppies, all trying to jump on her.

"Enough shouting." Siobhan grabbed the smallest boy and held him close. "You sound like a bunch of hooligans. Welcome, Laura. Mandy. We're glad you're here."

"Thank you for inviting us." How soon would it be polite to leave?

"These two monsters are Mary Kate's." She touched the oldest girl and the boy who looked about Mandy's age. "Shawna and Michael." She squeezed the smaller boy. "And this is Seth's little boy, Davy."

The front door opened into a large, comfortable, slightly shabby living room. The adults all seemed to be gathered around the fireplace. All of them were looking at her.

Siobhan led her forward and began introducing them. Mandy stayed close behind her, clutching her hand tightly. Most of them she knew already, but she hadn't met Brendan's wife or Seth's fiancée. She nodded, smiled, and decided that there were way too many Flanagans.

One was missing, though. She'd recognized the moment she entered the room that Ryan wasn't here. On duty, maybe? Before she could be sure whether she felt relief or disappointment, he came striding in from what was probably the kitchen.

She absolutely would not feel pleasure at the sight of him. Still, when his smile lit his deep-blue eyes, it was hard not to, especially when he came directly to her.

"Laura, hi. Well, what do you think?" He waved toward his family. "If you can stand all these people talking at once, you might be able to get through a Sunday supper at the Flanagan house."

"Stop teasing, Ryan." Siobhan swatted at him affectionately. "You make Laura feel welcome, now. I've got to get back to the roast."

"Can I do something—" she began, but Siobhan was already gone.

"This is your first time here," Ryan said. "Relax and enjoy yourself. It's Mary Kate's family's turn to help this week, anyway."

"You do this every Sunday?"

"Terrifying, isn't it?" His grin negated the words. "If the weather's nice, we go out to Gabe and Nolie's farm instead, where the kids can run. Mandy would like seeing the place. Lots of animals."

Was that an invitation? She wasn't sure, and maybe it was safer to ignore it.

"I thought maybe you were working tonight." That suggested she'd been looking for him, and she wanted the words back.

"We all try to get off Sunday when we can. These get-togethers are important to Mom. Besides, Pastor Brendan would get after us if we missed church." His eyebrows lifted. "I thought maybe we'd see you there this morning."

Apparently the Flanagans didn't intend to let her forget that she'd once belonged to their church. A little flicker of annoyance went through her. "I'm not sure Mandy would feel comfortable there."

"Why not?" His eyes were fixed on hers, seeming to demand an answer.

"It's difficult when she can't understand what's going on." And why won't you leave it alone?

"Nolie's always in church school. I know she'd be glad to sign for Mandy."

He was crowding her on the subject, and she frowned at him. "It's hard for her to interact with hearing children."

"Really?" He nodded toward the corner of the room. "She seems to be doing fine at the moment."

She'd thought Mandy was still at her side. Instead she was clear across the room, sitting in front of a tower of blocks with the other children.

She made an instinctive movement toward them. "I'll just go and—"

Ryan stopped her with a touch on her arm. "Why don't you let them play? They're okay."

Irritation scraped along her nerves. Ryan didn't know anything about raising a hearing-impaired child. But she watched as Shawna handed Mandy a block, clapping when she put it on top of the tower. Mandy's solemn little face broke into a smile.

Laura's throat tightened. That was what she wanted for Mandy—to see her playing normally with other children instead of being trapped and isolated in her silent world.

"Laura, it's grand to have you back in Suffolk." Ryan's father approached with an outstretched hand. She probably would have known Joe Flanagan anywhere—he still had that square, bulldog face and friendly smile, although only a few tinges of red showed in his now-white hair.

"Thank you. And thanks for all the help from your family with the fire clean-up."

He shrugged. "Firefighters enjoy seeing things put back to rights after a fire. You know that all of us Flanagans are involved with the department now, don't you?"

Ryan groaned. "Please, Dad. I'm sure Laura doesn't want to hear about our old family traditions."

His father's face tightened, as if he were about to issue a reprimand.

"I have every reason to know about Seth and Terry and Ryan, since I met them on the job," she said quickly.

Joe nodded. "I guess you did at that. Sorry I wasn't there. I never thought I'd be stuck at a desk job in the department, but it makes me proud to know that those three are out there on my old team."

She nodded, glancing at Ryan, and was struck by the expression that crossed his face at his father's words. What was it? It was gone too quickly to say, but she was left with a sense of something uneasy behind Ryan's smile.

Chapter Three

Despite her qualms, Laura decided that the evening had gone pretty well. They'd moved past dessert and coffee, and she sat next to Nolie, Gabe's wife, on the sofa. The other woman had the serene, absorbed face some women wore during pregnancy, as if they listened to something inside themselves.

"Do you know yet if the baby's a boy or girl? Or aren't you telling?"

She'd been eager to find out when she was pregnant. The tests had told her she was going to have a daughter. They hadn't been able to predict that Mandy would be born with a serious hearing problem.

"It's a girl." Nolie's face curved in a satisfied smile. "I thought maybe Gabe would want a boy first, but he says after growing up with his brothers and cousin, he's delighted to have a baby girl."

"That's lovely." Unexpected tears stung her eyes, and she blinked them away. "My husband—"

She stopped. Jason had been disappointed their child had been a girl, and doubly disappointed that she hadn't been perfect, but she shouldn't say that.

"I'm sorry." Nolie clasped her hand in sudden empathy, seeming to understand what she didn't say. "But you shouldn't worry too much about her. I work with children who have disabilities, so I see the parents' concerns all the time. Mandy's such a bright, loved child. Believe me, she'll do fine."

"I want her to have the best. I know she can live a full life without hearing, but if she qualifies for the cochlear implant—"

A cry interrupted her, and she swung around, heartbeat accelerating. Mandy—

Michael was trying to pull a toy train from her hand. He wrenched it free, and Mandy wailed.

She was across the room in an instant, but Siobhan got there first, pulling her grandson away.

"Michael Joseph Driscoll, I'm disappointed in you. Mandy is our guest. Say you're sorry."

"He just wanted to show her how it works, Grammy," Shawna said. "Honest."

Laura wrapped her arms around Mandy, feeling her child's hot tears against her face. Her heart hurt. Mandy didn't understand. How could she?

"Sorry," Michael mumbled.

Everyone was looking at them. All she wanted to do was get out.

"That's fine, Michael. I know you didn't mean it." She struggled to smile at the child. After all, he was just behaving like a normal, hearing five-year-old.

She stood, holding Mandy in her arms, arranging a smile on her face for Siobhan. "Mandy's getting tired. I think it's time we headed for home. Thank you so much for dinner."

Siobhan was wise enough not to argue, but Laura could read the regret in her eyes. She gave Laura a quick hug and stroked Mandy's curls. "It was lovely to have you here. Come again soon."

She nodded, her smile stiff. No, they wouldn't come again. All the Flanagans meant well, but Mandy needed a less chaotic environment than the one they provided.

Ryan reached her and lifted Mandy from her arms before she realized what he was doing. "I'll walk you out."

"I'll take her." They'd had this conversation before, hadn't they? Ryan hadn't listened to her then.

"Mandy's fine with me, aren't you, little girl?" He stroked Mandy's hair with a gentle touch.

She hated to admit it, but he was right. Mandy snuggled against him, her face tucked into his strong shoulder. For some reason that was obscure to Laura, Mandy trusted him.

She said her goodbyes quickly, trying to evade repeated invitations and offers of help from each of the Flanagans. It seemed the goodbyes would never end, but finally she escaped out the front door with Ryan carrying Mandy.

She paused for an instant on the porch, inhaling the cool spring air and absorbing the quiet.

"Okay?" Ryan gave her a quizzical look.

She could hardly tell him that his family exhausted

her. "Fine." She gave him a meaningless smile and walked quickly to the steps, eager to put this evening behind her.

They went down the steps in silence, the warm spring night closing around them. The porch light cast a yellow glow on the walk, fading as they neared the car.

She swung the rear door open, struggling to find something polite and dismissive to say to Ryan.

"She is tired, isn't she?" Ryan lowered Mandy to her booster seat and fastened the seatbelt carefully. He picked up the teddy bear. It looked tiny in his big hands as he tucked it against Mandy. "She's almost asleep already," he said softly.

Guilt flickered. "I shouldn't have stayed so long. This was too much excitement for her."

Ryan straightened, planting one hand against the car roof and looking at her questioningly. "Hey, I know we're a noisy bunch, but we're not that bad, are we?"

"I didn't mean it that way." She could feel the heat in her cheeks. She hadn't intended her words as an insult. He should realize that.

"It looked to me as if Mandy had a good time. Sure you're not overreacting a little?"

She stiffened. "If you're saying I'm overprotective of my daughter—"

"Hey, relax. I wasn't criticizing." He glanced at Mandy, asleep now with the bear cuddled against her chin, safe in the cocoon of her car seat. "I'd probably feel exactly the same if I were Mandy's parent."

Her flicker of anger died. "Maybe I am a little too

protective." The fact that he'd agreed with her made it easier to admit. "I just—well, I know I'm all Mandy has, so I have to do it right. I guess I still haven't figured out how to let her learn without getting hurt."

"Maybe that's impossible." He leaned toward her a little, and she caught the fresh scent of soap on his skin, mingled with the heady aroma of lilacs from the huge old bushes that flanked the driveway. "I don't know how my folks managed with the five of us, and then taking in my cousin Brendan, too. We were always getting hurt."

"Your parents had each other to rely on." Her thoughts flickered to Jason. She'd learned the hard way not to rely on him.

"Even with a ton of family around willing to give you free advice, it's not always easy to know what to do."

His serious expression startled her. She wasn't used to seeing somber reflection from Ryan, and she'd guess most other people weren't, either. He was always so laughing and relaxed that it was hard to remember that he probably had his dark moments, too.

"Have they been giving you advice about something?"

Somehow the dusk and quiet of the warm summer evening made it easier to ask the personal question. It was as if, for the moment at least, they were enclosed together, separate from the happy, noisy family group she knew was behind the wide windows.

He shook his head. "Actually, this time I haven't let them in on it. Sometimes other people's expectations get in the way of knowing what's best for you."

"Is it something you want to talk about?"

"Are you offering to listen?" He leaned a little closer, until she could almost feel his breath against her face.

Her heart lurched. It took an effort to speak evenly.

"After everything you've done for us, listening is a small repayment."

"No repayment needed. But actually, I'm thinking of making a career change."

That startled her. "Leave the fire department?" She'd imagine that would create a stir in the Flanagan family. They'd all seemed so proud of their position. Even Brendan, the minister, was the fire department chaplain, he'd told her.

"Not leave entirely, no. I've applied for a position with the arson squad. It's run by the fire department here in Suffolk, rather than the police like it is some places, but it's a separate branch."

"Is that really such a change? You'd still be a firefighter in a way, wouldn't you?"

"You heard my dad. He's so proud that Seth and Terry and I are in his old squad." He frowned, his dark brows creating a V. "He had a hard time adjusting when Gabe got hurt and couldn't fight fire anymore, and then his heart attack took him off the line."

"You don't want to disappoint him." She understood, only too well, and was surprised at the similarity to her own life. She'd gladly have gone into the construction business with her father, but her mother wouldn't hear of it. "He'd want you to do what was right for you, wouldn't he?"

Ryan's smile flickered. "He thinks he already knows what that is."

"And you're not so sure anymore."

"I never considered any other line of work." He shrugged. "I don't know. Maybe I'm looking for a different challenge. Or maybe I'm just trying to get out from under my big brothers' shadows."

She didn't know what to say. She'd always thought Ryan Flanagan one of those lucky beings who are born confident, laughing and sure of himself. Now it looked as if he had doubts, too.

She felt for him—a sudden empathy that startled and disturbed her. She didn't want to feel for anyone but her daughter. She had far too much responsibility in her life right now to leave room for anything else.

Luckily he didn't seem to expect an answer from her. He touched her arm lightly, and she felt the warmth of that touch right through the fabric of her sweater.

"Hey, I'll work it out. But thanks for listening. I'll be glad to return the favor, any time."

She managed to smile, to nod. Ryan meant well, but she didn't have any intention of sharing her inner thoughts with anyone, least of all him. He'd come too far into her life already.

Now what exactly was he doing back here again? Ryan didn't have a good answer to that question as he approached Laura's building the next day. If those moments with Laura by her car the night before had taught him anything, it was that she spelled danger to a man like him.

He ought to stay as far away as possible from Laura

McKay, with her fierce sense of responsibility and her prickly determination to do everything herself. Instead here he was, putting his head in the front door that stood ajar, probably to air the place out.

"Anybody home?" He tapped on the frame.

Mandy's head jerked up. Had she responded to the sound or the vibration? He wasn't sure. She had a child's toy broom and dustpan, and she'd obviously been mimicking her mother's work.

"Hi, Mandy."

She broke into a smile and carefully finger-spelled his name.

"Good job."

"What's a good job?" Laura came in from the kitchen, carrying a bucket. "Hi, Ryan."

"Mandy finger-spelled my name when I came in."

A smile blazed across Laura's face. "That is a good job." She set the bucket on the floor and hugged the little girl, and for a moment the love in her eyes seemed strong enough to light the world.

It was a warning, that love. It announced in no uncertain terms that he couldn't wander into their lives and then wander out again. Laura and Mandy needed more than that.

I'm just helping out, he told his conscience firmly. Nothing else.

"You're making progress." He glanced around the large rectangular room that was cleared now of debris. The fireplace that covered most of one wall had obviously just been cleaned, revealing the mellow, rosy tone of the bricks.

"Not enough." Laura followed the direction of his gaze, but her level brows drew down, as if she saw all that remained to be done instead of what she'd accomplished already. "The fire put me days behind my schedule."

"I can spare some time to help on my off days, if you want."

The corners of her wide mouth tucked in, as if she didn't want to give anything away. "That's not necessary. I can—"

"I know. You can do it yourself. That doesn't mean an extra pair of hands wouldn't make it go faster."

She evaded his eyes, and he suspected she was searching for a good excuse. Or at least, a change of subject.

"Maybe so." Her tone was noncommittal. "Tell me, have you talked to your folks yet about the new job?"

She'd opted for the change of subject. And he must have been suffering from a mental lapse when he'd told her about that. Why on earth would he talk to her about something he hadn't even told his family?

"Not yet, but I have to." He couldn't suppress a grin. "I just heard that I passed the test. I've been called for an interview."

And once again, he'd told her something he'd told no one else.

She came closer, as if she needed to study his face seriously. "Are you happy about it?"

Was he? A good question. "I guess. The arson squad would be a challenge, if I got it. Lots of brainwork." He grimaced. "To tell the truth, I'm better at physical challenges than mental ones."

Maybe that was the problem. He liked the physical risks of firefighting, maybe too much. He'd told Laura about Dad's heart attack, but he hadn't told her all of it. Not about the part he'd played.

"Just tell them." She put her hand lightly on his arm. "They might surprise you. And if they're upset, at least it will be out in the open. You can't deal with it as long as they don't know."

"You're pretty good in the advice department, you know that?"

She smiled slightly, shaking her head. "I should have learned something from all the mistakes I've made."

A man who was interested in a woman would follow up on a comment like that. But he'd just told himself how wrong it would be to get interested in her, hadn't he? Whatever he said next had to be noncommittal.

"Well, given the way rumors fly around the department, I'd better come clean before they hear it from someone else."

Laura didn't move, but she seemed to draw back a little. Her smile faded. She got the message.

She turned her attention to the bucket, wringing a sponge out as if it were a very important action. "Speaking of the department, I'd say you've more than done your duty here. The fire damage is cleaned up, and I'm back on target with my renovation."

It was a nice, polite dismissal. Well, that was what he wanted, wasn't it? He couldn't get involved with her. He couldn't let Mandy start to depend on him. Everyone knew he wasn't dependable when it came to relationships.

He took a breath. For some reason, he couldn't seem to find the words to agree with her. "I'll just check that back door to be sure the new lock is in right, and then I'll be on my way."

She nodded, her smile stiff.

Right. He headed for the kitchen before he could say something he shouldn't.

Fifteen minutes later he was still fiddling with a perfectly good lock. Maybe he ought to face the fact that he didn't want to leave.

This isn't about what you want, dummy. It's about what's the right thing to do.

His head came up at the sound of voices in the other room. Apparently Laura had company.

"Mr. Potter." Laura didn't sound happy to be interrupted yet again.

"Bradley, please. I thought you were going to call me Bradley."

Bradley Potter. Nice, well-off, the last son of one of Suffolk's founding families. Brad was a successful businessman, good-looking, single. Laura ought to be friendlier to someone like that.

"Another list of changes?" She didn't sound particularly friendly at the moment. He heard the rustle of papers. "But I've already complied with the requirements from the historic preservation committee."

"I'm so sorry." Bradley's tone exuded sympathy. "I wish I didn't have to bring you bad news, but I'm sure you understand that we have to be very careful about any renovations that go on in the historic district."

"I know that." Laura snapped the words.

Maybe he'd better get in there before she got into a fight with one of the most influential men in town. He strolled into the room, enjoying the look of surprise on Brad's face at the sight of him.

"Hey, Brad. What are you up to?"

"Ryan. What are you doing here?" Brad nodded stiffly, his immaculate dress shirt and flannel pants incongruous in what was essentially a construction site.

Still, he was a lot better for Laura and Mandy than a commitment-phobic firefighter.

"Just checking up on some of the repairs after the fire. You did know that Ms. McKay had a fire out in the back, didn't you?"

"I heard." Brad turned toward Laura. "I'm so sorry for all the trouble you've been having." He nodded toward the papers in her hand. "And that I have to add to your problems at a time like this."

Mandy came to lean against Ryan, and he put one hand on her shoulder. Maybe the child sensed the tension in the room and had picked him for a friend. Laura certainly looked as if she'd gotten some bad news.

"So how exactly are you adding to Ms. McKay's problems?" Stay out of it, he told himself. But he didn't seem to be listening.

Laura looked up from the papers, her face pale and tight. "The historic preservation committee has landed me with a new set of requirements. Two pages' worth of things they didn't tell me on the initial inspection."

"As I was saying to Laura, the preservation committee is especially careful of any renovation in the historic district." Brad's tone was as smooth as silk. He must have practiced that statement a few times. "I might personally think they're being a little unreasonable, but I have to do as the committee tells me."

"Let me have a look at what they're asking." He reached for the papers.

But before he could reach them, Brad took them from Laura's hands. "This is just a work sheet. I'll have a more official list drawn up and drop it off for you."

"Thank you." Her voice was tight.

Brad seemed to hesitate, glancing from Ryan to Laura. "Look, I know these changes seem unduly harsh. Why don't I have a word with the committee members unofficially, before this goes to its final format? Maybe I can get them to ease up on some of their requirements."

"Would you?" Laura's smile blazed, and Brad blinked as if the sun had just come out.

"Of course." His voice warmed suddenly. "Of course I would."

Hadn't he been telling himself that Brad Potter was just the sort of man for Laura? He shouldn't feel like punching the guy just because Laura was looking at him as if he were some sort of hero.

Laura hadn't seen much of the Flanagans for several days, and nothing at all of Ryan. She ran the paint roller smoothly along the downstairs wall, admiring the rich burgundy she'd decided on after researching the original colors.

The floor refinishing had gone beautifully, and now that she could get the paint on the walls, this area was really shaping up. It would be perfect for a small shop catering to the visitors in the historic district or a lovely living room for a buyer who wanted a private home.

Nolie Flanagan had enthused about the color when she'd stopped by earlier. She'd come with an invitation for Mandy to visit the farm and see the animals.

Laura had been evasive. Mandy would love to see the animals, of course, but she couldn't help thinking it was better not to get too involved with the Flanagan family. She didn't want to be anyone's object of charity, no matter how sincere they were.

She frowned at the fresh paint. She ought to be honest with herself, at least. The truth was that she should stay away from them because she found herself far too attracted to Ryan's easy smile for her peace of mind.

All she could concentrate on right now was Mandy's welfare. There was no room in her life for anything else. She was happy Ryan hadn't been around. So why did she feel so out of sorts?

She glanced at her watch. The plasterers were supposed to be here by now to do the third-floor walls. That was one thing she hadn't felt competent to tackle herself. She put down the roller and stretched. Maybe she'd better take a break and call the plasterer.

Five minutes later she returned the phone to the cradle carefully, because if she didn't, she just might throw the receiver against the wall. She clutched her hair with her hands, heedless of the paint she was probably spreading around, and squeezed her eyes closed. What else could possibly go wrong?

"What's the matter?" The voice came like an echo of her thoughts.

She swung around, blinking back tears. She wouldn't give in to that weakness, especially not in front of Ryan.

"Hi. I didn't hear you come in." And why did she always have to look like a total wreck whenever Ryan saw her?

He crossed the room toward her, his gaze fixed on her face. "Something's wrong. What?"

She shook her head, appalled at how glad she was to see him. "Plasterers. They were supposed to show up today. Instead they're suddenly so busy that they can't possibly squeeze me in for at least a couple of weeks."

"You can't wait a couple of weeks?"

"Impossible. I have to get this done." She could hear her voice veering out of control, and she couldn't seem to help it. "If I'm not finished by the time my prospective buyer comes, she'll go elsewhere. And Mandy's surgery—"

She stopped, fighting for control. She wasn't going to spill all her troubles to Ryan, no matter how sympathetic he was.

And then he touched her shoulder gently, and all her resolve disappeared. She choked on a sob, and he pulled her against him.

"Don't." She tried ineffectually to move away. "You'll get paint on your shirt."

"It'll clean." His arms were strong around her, demanding nothing, just offering support. He stroked her back in gentle circles, reminding her of the way she comforted Mandy. "Just relax. You don't have to be a superhero all the time."

She wanted to protest that she did, but it was so comforting to stand in his embrace, feeling the tension easing out of her at his touch. His lips brushed her temple.

That touch brought her to her senses. She sucked in a breath and drew back, still in the circle of his arms. "Sorry. I don't usually do that."

"You're allowed." His gaze probed. "Let me get this straight. You need the money from the sale of the property to pay for Mandy's surgery."

She nodded, pulling herself free and turning away from that intent gaze. "The insurance we have doesn't cover a cochlear implant."

"If you waited on the surgery until you're in better shape financially—"

"No." Again her tone veered upward, and she fought to control it. "We're not going to wait. The longer Mandy goes without the implant, the harder it will be. She starts school in September. I have to give her every chance at a hearing life. I have to."

"Okay." He probably hoped that calm tone of his would soothe her. "Seems like the first step is to get a plasterer in here, ASAP."

She was glad he'd given her an excuse to be annoyed with him. "I never thought of that."

He grinned. "Sarcasm will get you nowhere, lady. It just so happens one of my high-school buddies recently took over his father's plastering business. I'll call him."

"He'll probably be booked solid. They all are." It had taken her weeks to find someone, and Ryan proposed to do it with a single call.

"Trust me, he'll fit you in. I know too much about him for him to say no to me."

Hope flickered in spite of her doubts. "That would be wonderful."

"Looks like it's a good thing I stopped by today, although I didn't have plasterers in mind."

"Why did you come, then?"

"I thought you'd want to know." His smile broadened. "I got the call. I've been assigned to the arson squad on a probationary basis."

"Ryan, congratulations. That's wonderful."

"Yeah, it is. I didn't realize how much I wanted this until it came through. I'm going to be working with Garrett North. He's tough, but he's the best."

He was as enthusiastic as a kid with a new toy, and she couldn't help smiling with him.

"I take it you've told your family. How are they taking it?"

He waggled his hand. "So-so. Not as bad as I thought, actually."

"That's good. I'm really happy for you."

"Well, there's something you should know before you get too happy." The sudden serious turn of his expression made her nerves tighten in response.

"What is it?" Something told her she wouldn't like his answer.

"I've been assigned to my first investigation. It's here." He gestured. "Your fire wasn't an accident. It was arson."

Chapter Four

Laura could only stare at Ryan, her mind slowly processing his words. The fire here. Arson.

She finally found the words. "Someone deliberately set the fire? That's impossible." She couldn't believe it. He had to be wrong about this.

"I'm sorry. I know you don't want to hear news like that. Nobody does."

She was shaking her head, as if that would change his opinion. Groping for another explanation.

"You said yourself that the construction debris was a hazard on the back porch. Remember? It must have been an accident."

It must have been, because the alternative was too frightening to think about.

"Look, let's sit down and talk about this." He touched her arm, nodding toward the stairs. "You're having a lot of stuff thrown at you lately. I'm sorry to add to it."

He sounded like Bradley Potter with his list of bad news. She shook off the thought. Unlike Bradley, Ryan was just leveling with her. She ought to appreciate that, even if she thought he was wrong.

She let him pilot her to the stairwell, and they sat on the worn wooden treads. Deep burgundy stair carpeting, she thought automatically. She'd already picked it out.

But she couldn't waste time daydreaming about something that was already done. She had to face this new problem rationally.

"What makes you and this other investigator think it was arson?" She didn't even like saying the word, with its implication of malice.

"We know an accelerant was spread around the porch." He said the words slowly, as if to be sure she understood. "It leaves traces."

"An accelerant."

"Probably paint thinner." He glanced toward the open paint cans in the front room. "Do you have any around?"

She stiffened. Was he accusing her of carelessness? "I do, but it's locked up in the cellar. No one could have gotten at it."

Ryan leaned back against the newel post. The pose might be casual, but the way he studied her face was serious. "They didn't have to find it here. They could have brought it with them."

"They." She didn't want to picture faceless people spreading paint thinner, striking a match. "Why would anyone want to destroy something I've been working so hard on? It doesn't make any sense."

"Plenty of things in this world don't make sense. This could have been a gang of kids, tempted by the stuff, not realizing the danger."

"Not realizing! We were asleep upstairs." Dread moved like a cold draft on her neck.

His hand closed over hers, gripping it strongly. "I know. But kids may not have known someone was living in the building. It's been empty a long time."

A shudder ran through her. Ryan's fingers tightened on hers as if he felt it, too.

"Look, if that is what happened, we'll probably never find them unless somebody talks. They'll have been scared to death by what happened. You can be sure they'd never willingly come near here again."

"I guess I should find that comforting."

"Well, I'm trying to put the best light on it I can." The stroke of his thumb across her knuckles was feather-light. "I don't like being the bearer of bad news, believe me."

She managed a smile. Ryan didn't deserve to have her worries dumped on him. He had enough to think about with his new job. She wasn't his responsibility.

"Okay. I promise not to overreact to the news. But I am glad you're investigating."

"I doubt Lieutenant North will let me do anything more responsible than carry his notebook, but at least I'll get my feet wet." His eyes were serious. "North is the best. I couldn't ask for anyone better to train under."

"Then I know my case is getting excellent attention."

Did his family see how much Ryan wanted to succeed at this? They should be proud that he was attempting something so difficult.

"There is one other thing—"

He looked so reluctant to speak that for a moment her fear rose again. Then she realized what he hesitated to tell her.

"I suppose it's a conflict of interest for you to be friends with me under the circumstances. I can understand that."

That meant he wouldn't be dropping in on her anymore. Well, that was probably for the best. She'd already decided on that, hadn't she?

He smiled. "Actually, that's not an issue. When I told North that we're old friends, that we'd been in school together, he just rolled his eyes. Said he was beginning to think everyone in Suffolk knew everyone else. I guess it's a big change for him from Chicago."

"That's not quite true."

He blinked. "What isn't?"

She said the thing she'd been thinking since the day Ryan had walked back into her life. "That we were friends in school. You barely knew who I was in those days."

"Just because we weren't in the same class—"

"That didn't have anything to do with it. You dated girls in my class. We weren't friends because you were the football hero and I was the shy little nerd who hid behind my stack of library books."

He looked down at their clasped hands. "You're telling me I was a jerk, in other words."

Heat flooded her face. "No, of course not. I'm just saying we didn't run in the same circles. I was so far from the in crowd I probably didn't have a circle."

"Why?"

Now it was her turn to blink. "Why what?"

"Why did you hide?"

Nerd. Loner. He could have used those words, but he wouldn't because he was too kind. Maybe he didn't remember what it had been like in high school for the kids who didn't belong to that charmed circle of the accepted. Maybe he hadn't even known.

"I was shy," she said carefully. "I didn't have any confidence in myself." She wasn't going to talk to Ryan, of all people, about how it had felt growing up with her mother's disappointments hanging over her.

He cradled her hand between both of his. "You know, it's a funny thing. Every day I run into people I went to high school with. Most of them are still the same people they were then—still replaying old games. But you—you've turned into someone completely different."

The touch of his hands seemed to be turning her insides to jelly and her brain to mush. She struggled to treat the words lightly, because if she showed how his opinion mattered to her, she'd be betraying too much.

"You mean I don't qualify as a nerd any longer?"

His gaze was serious and intent. "I mean you've grown into a woman who's a dozen times better than that in crowd. Strong. Independent. Capable. Ready to tackle anything for your child. I'd say that's a pretty good comeback."

The lump in her throat wouldn't let her say much. "Thank you." It came out as a whisper, and she cleared her throat, embarrassed.

"Just remember that when you have to battle the likes of Bradley Potter."

"The consummate member of the in crowd? I will."

Ryan released her hand and pushed to his feet. He stood for a moment, hand on the newel post, looking down at her.

"There was something else I wanted to say. Before I got sidetracked by our high-school social status."

A chill crept down her spine. "What?"

"The arson very likely was what I said. Kids, out to make mischief and going too far." His face clouded. "But according to North, we can't rule out the possibility that we're looking for a firebug."

The expression on his face told her he was serious. "Have there been other fires?"

"Not recently." His frown deepened. "But about five years ago we had a rash of fires in the business district. No one was hurt, but there was a lot of property damage. They never caught the guy."

"The fires just stopped?"

He nodded. "That's not unusual. That kind of person can go for years and then break out again."

She struggled to remember what she knew about firebugs. "They come back sometimes, don't they? If they set a fire and it's put out, they might try again."

"It's possible." He leaned over to grasp her shoulder. "Look, I didn't tell you that because I wanted to scare you. Chances are good it's nothing of the kind. But I know you weren't in Suffolk when that happened before, and I thought you ought to know."

She straightened her spine. "You were right to tell me." She looked up at him, hoping she didn't look panicked. "Do you think we're safe here? Mandy—" Her throat closed at the thought of her daughter.

"Whoever set the fire knows now that someone lives here. I think that'll discourage him."

"Unless he wants to hurt someone." She couldn't help the shiver of fear, but she tried to keep it out of her voice.

"If it is the same person, he was always careful to pick empty buildings. Still, I've thought of a couple things that might be good precautions." He eyed her cautiously, as if wondering how much advice she'd willingly take from him.

"What things?" If it meant Mandy's safety, she'd take advice from anyone.

He looked faintly relieved at her response. "Lights on the back of the building, first off, because the alley is so dark. Motion detector lights would be best. Maybe you ought to consider an alarm system."

Those things cost money she didn't have. Still, she'd have to find a way to pay for them if that meant keeping her daughter safe.

"I'll look into it right away."

"Seth and I can probably install the lights for you." He grinned. "We once rigged the doorbell to ring every time Gabe turned on the light in his room. Drove him crazy until he figured out what we'd done."

Ryan was trying to dispel her fears, and she appreciated that. He was definitely one of the good guys, no matter who he'd been in high school.

Unfortunately the fear wouldn't be chased away so easily, no matter what he said. Somehow she thought she wouldn't be sleeping well for quite a while.

"There's little enough left to find now that half the town of Suffolk has trampled through here."

Lieutenant North stood in the alley with Ryan the next day, glaring at the back porch of Laura's building. The area was as clean as a burned-out porch could be after the ministrations of the Flanagan crew.

"Sorry." Ryan shifted his weight, wondering how much he should confess. He wanted to impress North with his ability to solve the crime, not cover up the evidence. "Some people from the church came over to help clean up. There was no thought of arson at the time."

"No." North glanced around, his shrewd gray eyes seeming to see the alleyway as it must have been that night. "No one thought of it until the anonymous call came in." He frowned, lines deepening in his lean face. "I don't like anonymous callers."

Tipsters were useful sometimes, but Ryan understood what North meant. Someone out there had knowledge, and maybe it was guilty knowledge.

"If kids did this, you'd hardly expect them to draw attention to the fact that it was arson by placing the call." That fact had been worrying Ryan from the moment he'd heard about the tip.

North gave a grudging nod, as if to concede that Ryan did have a brain. "A firebug, on the other hand, might resent the fact that his talent was overlooked."

The firebug. Ryan had been a rookie in the department then, but he remembered only too well the tension of knowing an arsonist was on the loose in his town. Every shift he'd been keyed up, worrying that this time the firebug might miscalculate and kill someone.

"You think something's set the same guy off again?" Ryan couldn't help but ask the question, even though North wasn't likely to answer.

"I think we don't overlook anything." North's tone suggested that he wasn't going to speculate with a junior officer.

"Right." What did North think they'd overlooked to begin with? It really bugged Ryan that they hadn't even suspected arson that morning.

North pointed with his pen to the buildings that lined the opposite side of the alley. "The first thing is we talk to everyone who might have seen something."

"The police already—" Ryan began.

"We don't accept someone else's investigation, Flanagan. The fact that you probably personally know the investigating officer doesn't mean anything to me. We do it again."

"Yes. Right." He wasn't exactly doing a sterling job of impressing the man on his first morning on the job. "I'll get started on that."

The back door of the house creaked open. Laura looked out at them, her eyes wary at their presence. "Ryan. What's going on?"

"I'm sorry if we disturbed you. We're checking out the scene of the fire."

"I see." Laura's gaze was guarded as she glanced at Lieutenant North.

He took a step closer. The shadows under Laura's eyes were darker today, her stance more tense. The news he'd given her about the arson investigation had probably kept her up most of the night.

"You look like you had a rough night of it."

She grimaced. "Jumping at every sound, I'm afraid."

"I'm sorry."

"Not your fault."

No point in saying he wished he hadn't had to bring her the bad news.

"I did get the lights you recommended," she said. "And someone from the church called to say he had an alarm system he could put in for me at cost." Her eyebrows lifted. "I take it you've been interfering again."

"Hey, don't blame me because people want to help you. Just accept it."

"Not when I can't repay them." Her jaw tensed. "That's not right."

"Has anyone even told you that there's a difference between being independent and being just plain stubborn?"

Anger flared in her face, but he just shook his head.

"I don't have time to fight with you, Laura. I'm on duty. If you want to get to know the people from church who helped you, just go to service on Sunday. They'll be glad to know that their friendship brought you there."

She still looked ready to argue, but apparently she realized this wasn't the time. She swung the door partly closed.

"I'll let you get back to work." There was a snap in her voice.

Right. She didn't like his advice. Well, fine. The best thing he could do for Laura was to accomplish this task and find the arsonist. Let her make her own decisions about accepting help.

He spun on his heel. North stood several feet away, notebook in his hand. But he wasn't looking at the notebook. He was looking toward Laura with a cool, almost inhuman assessment in his eyes.

A wave of emotion swept over Ryan, so strong it almost rocked him back on his heels. He wanted to step between that look and Laura. Wanted to protect her from anything and anyone that might threaten her.

Whoa, back off. He wasn't interested in commitment, remember?

Besides, Laura had made it only too clear that she didn't appreciate his interference in her life. Feeling anything stronger than friendship toward her could only lead to complications neither of them wanted.

"Are you sure this is a good idea?" Seth shot a glance at Ryan as they turned down Laura's street that evening. "Laura didn't exactly say she wanted our help, did she?"

"If we wait for Laura to say she needs help, we'll both be old and gray." He gripped the steering wheel tighter. Laura needed assistance, from them or someone else, whether she was willing to admit it or not.

"What if she tells us to take a hike?"

"Then I turn on the famous Flanagan charm." He

grinned at his sober older brother. "You're just jealous because it skipped you."

"I have Julie. I don't need to charm other women, thanks very much."

No, Seth didn't. He had, somewhat to his surprise, found the love of his life where he least expected her, and he and his Julie were so happy in love that it almost made a man think he ought to try getting engaged, too. Almost.

Ryan pulled to the curb in front of the brick building. "I'll talk her into it. You'll see."

Seth raised an eyebrow. "Maybe you will, at that. Has it occurred to you to wonder why you're so intent on helping this woman?"

"Because it's the right thing to do."

"Yeah, right." Seth slid out of the car and followed him to the door. "Not because you're interested in her, by any chance?"

Ryan gritted his teeth, trying to ignore the comment as he rang the bell.

"Well?" Seth's soft-voiced question made it clear he wouldn't give up easily.

"Mind your own business, big brother." He treated Seth to a glare. "I don't need any advice."

"Maybe not, but—"

The door swung open, and Seth shut up. But judging from the mulish set to his jaw, he wasn't finished. That was the trouble with older brothers. They never stopped thinking they had the right to give you advice.

"Ryan." Laura sounded more resigned than surprised. "What brings you here tonight?"

He hefted his toolbox. "We're here to install the lights. You remember my brother Seth, don't you?"

She nodded to Seth. "I also remember telling you I could handle the installation myself."

"Why would you want to, when you've got two willing helpers standing on your doorstep?" He tried the smile that usually softened female hearts. "Aren't you going to at least ask us in?"

Laura didn't look noticeably softened, but she did step back.

"Wow, this looks great." Seth looked around the freshly-painted room. The rich burgundy on the walls glowed softly against the pristine white woodwork. "You're really making progress."

"Thanks." Her face relaxed in a smile. "Actually, the place is starting to look so good that I'll hate to part with it."

"Your buyer's going to love what you've done," Ryan said. "How about the plastering? Did you get the arrangements made with my buddy?"

"Your friend is coming to do it in a few days." Unfortunately, that seemed to remind her that she owed him, or felt she owed him, for his help with the plasterer. Her smile vanished, to be replaced with a stubborn tightening of her jaw. "I have the lights under control."

"Are you telling us to go away?"

She blinked at the blunt question. "No, but—"

"Besides, you don't want to get into trouble with the fire inspector over the installation, do you?"

"You wouldn't."

He grinned, unrepentant. "Let us take care of the installation, and you'll never have to find out." He turned at the soft sound of footsteps on the stairs. "Hi, Mandy. I'm glad to see you."

His awkward signing brought a slight smile to the little girl's solemn face. She looked toward Seth.

"You remember my brother, don't you?"

She nodded. Then, to his surprise, she came to give him a hug.

He knelt, feeling her small arms tight around his neck, and discovered a lump in his throat. He looked up at Laura.

"You don't want Mandy to see us arguing, do you?"

The soft smile she had for her daughter seemed to include him. "I guess not."

Mandy signed something to her mother, too quick for him to catch. Laura hesitated a moment before nodding.

"Mandy wants you to come up and say good night before you leave." There might have been a faint flush on her cheeks at the words.

"Sure thing." He gave the child an okay sign, and she grinned.

"Why don't you both come up? I'll make some coffee, and we have homemade cookies."

He raised his eyebrows in exaggerated surprise. "You baked for us?"

"No. Your mother was here today." She gave a reluctant smile as she turned to follow her daughter up the stairs. "I couldn't turn her away, either. You'll find the new lights on the counter in the back room."

He waited until mother and daughter were out of sight before turning to Seth with a cocky grin. "See?"

Seth gave him a friendly push toward the door. "I see plenty. Let's get to work before it's too dark to figure out what we're doing."

Seth began unpacking the new lights, laying the pieces out neatly on the scarred countertop. That was Seth, always organized. He set his toolbox next to them and flipped it open.

"We'll need a ladder," Ryan said. "I want these fixtures high enough that no one can easily disable them. At least the motion lights are sensitive enough to let her know if anyone sets foot in that alley."

Seth nodded. "You're taking this plenty seriously, aren't you?"

A chill snaked down his spine. "I don't want to miscalculate. Not if we really have a firebug on the loose again."

Seth's face went grim. "I'm with you there. I remember what it was like. You think North is good enough to catch this guy?"

"He's good." He shot Seth a glance. "You might give your brother a little credit, though. I'm on the job, too, don't forget."

"Hah." Seth's scornful expression told him only too clearly what he thought of that. "Just don't make any rookie mistakes."

"I don't plan to. Not where Laura and Mandy's safety is concerned."

Seth planted his hands against the countertop. "Try not to make any rookie mistakes where Laura and that little girl's *happiness* is concerned, either."

Obviously Seth thought he was duty-bound to inter-fere, just like he always did.

"We're friends, okay? That's all."

Seth shrugged. "Just pointing out the problem. You can't do your usual love 'em and leave 'em routine when there's a child involved. That little girl could get hurt if she starts to depend on you."

"Especially since everyone in Suffolk seems to know how undependable I am." One thing about broth-ers—they knew how to hit you where it hurt.

"Look, bro, there's nobody I'd rather have backing me up on the fireground. You know that." Seth clapped him on the shoulder. "But emotional commitment's a whole other game. I'm just saying that this time, you've got to be careful."

"You don't need to worry." He tried to keep the ir-ritation out of his voice. Seth meant well, even if he was as clumsy as a bull in a china shop. "Laura's not look-ing for a relationship any more than I am."

Seth grinned, turning back to the lights. "Sometimes that's the most dangerous thing of all."

Chapter Five

Laura arranged a smile on her face and opened the apartment door to the Flanagan brothers. But only one Flanagan stood there, and it was Ryan. It was positively demoralizing how her stomach did a little flip at the sight of him. She might as well be fifteen again.

"Hi. All finished?"

He nodded. "You're now the proud possessor of motion-detector lights that will go on if so much as a stray cat enters the area behind the house."

"I'm not sure I'm worried about stray cats." She stepped back for him to enter and closed the door. Appalling, the way the man's height and breadth seemed to fill up her small living room.

"That is a disadvantage, I guess." He gave her that easy smile. "Actually I was exaggerating. We set them high enough that they shouldn't go on for anything that low to the ground. We didn't want to have you jumping out of bed to check every five minutes."

"Thank you. So much." She realized her hands were clenching and pressed them flat against her jeans. "What happened to your brother?"

"Seth was in a hurry to get home and see his fiancée." He shook his head. "Sad, the things that getting engaged do to a man."

Was there an edge to his voice on that subject? She wasn't sure.

"According to your mother, you've had quite a spate of marriages in your family in the past year." Siobhan had been clearly delighted about that fact when they'd chatted over the cookies that afternoon.

"It's pitiful. First Gabe, then my cousin Brendan, and next comes Seth."

"But not you."

"Hey, there has to be at least one Flanagan left to play the field."

"And you're the expert at that." At least, according to his mother he was.

He shrugged. "So they say." He raised an eyebrow at her. "You got married right out of college, I guess."

"Yes." She clipped the word off and then feared her short response had betrayed too much. "Jason and I met in college." And she'd been swept right off her feet by his assurance and the flattering attention he'd paid her.

"I'm sorry for your loss." Ryan's words were conventional, but his deep-blue gaze was intent, as if probing for what she didn't say.

"Thank you."

He was a charmer, like you, Ryan. Unfortunately there wasn't much character beneath the charm.

She cleared her throat. "Mandy's in bed already, but I'm sure she's still awake, waiting for you to say good night."

He flexed his fingers. "I've been practicing my sign language for the occasion."

"This way."

She was very aware of him close behind her as she led the way into Mandy's bedroom. The playful jungle animals in the mural she'd put on the far wall seemed to smile at them.

"Mandy, look who's come to say good night."

Mandy looked up from her book, her small face lighting with a smile. Her fingers formed the sign for R and brushed her chin.

Ryan glanced at her, eyebrows lifting. "Okay, I'm in trouble already. What does that mean?"

"It's a name sign. Mandy made it up for you. The letter R, touching her chin. For the cleft in your chin."

She hoped she wasn't blushing. Well, he must know the appeal that had for women of all ages, apparently.

"Oh." He looked disconcerted, and for a moment she actually thought he was the one who blushed. "That's really nice, Mandy." He went to sit next to her on the bed. "What are you reading? A book about puppies."

Mandy held the book out to him. That didn't need translation.

He took it. "You want me to read? I probably can't sign all the words."

"That's okay," Laura said. "I'll do the signing along with you."

Ryan nodded, putting the book on his lap so that he

and Mandy could both see it. He began to read, his deep voice a counterpoint to the hesitant movement of his hands.

Actually, he did pretty well with the signing. Either he knew more than he'd shown them so far, or he'd been getting some coaching.

The idea touched her, but it disturbed her almost as much. Ryan wasn't a part of their lives. She didn't want Mandy to begin to depend on him.

Still, she could hardly deny her child the opportunity to have friends just because those friends might not always be there. She struggled with the idea while she automatically signed the words to the short picture book.

"The end." Ryan closed the book and tucked it next to Mandy. "Good story."

She nodded, settling back on her pillow.

"Night-night, sweetheart." Laura bent over to kiss Mandy's soft cheek.

"Night. Sweet dreams." Ryan stood, his arm brushing Laura's warmly.

Breathe, she ordered herself, and got busy tucking the covers in and switching off the light. The room was bathed in the soft yellow glow of the nightlight, and the zebras and elephants smiled protectively.

"Sleep tight."

By the time they'd covered the few steps to the living room, Laura had managed to get her breathing under control. She turned to Ryan. "You've learned some more sign language, haven't you?"

"Nolie taught me." He shrugged it off. "It seems like a useful thing to know."

"I suppose." As long as that was all there was to it.

"By the way, she and Gabe have some new puppies at the farm. Since Mandy likes puppies so much, you ought to bring her out to see them."

"We'll see." That was a useful phrase for avoiding something she wasn't sure she wanted to do. "Please, sit down. I'll get the coffee."

The cups, sugar and cream were ready on a tray in the kitchen. All that remained was to set the coffeepot on its trivet. She had no excuse to delay going back to Ryan.

When she pushed back through the swinging door, she found he'd made himself comfortable on the couch.

He looked around the small room. "This is nice. I suppose you did it all yourself."

"Of course." She'd loved filling the apartment with the warm glow of chintz and patchwork, so different from the sterile modern furnishings her husband had preferred. She'd taken the red, white and blue color scheme in the living room from the patchwork quilt she'd thrown over the back of the couch to disguise the worn places.

"Thanks." He took the mug she handed him and snagged two cookies from the plate. "Chocolate peanut butter chip oatmeal. I'd recognize my mother's cookies anywhere."

"It was nice of her to bring them over." She hesitated. "She really seems to remember me from when she taught my church-school class. She mentioned a lot of things that happened when we were in high school."

"Mom has an encyclopedic memory for detail." He shuddered. "Especially for things you'd rather she forget. Did she bring up the time I got suspended for kidnapping Winston High's mascot before the homecoming game?"

She smiled. "As a matter of fact, she did. Said she never could understand why you did such a thing. I didn't enlighten her."

His eyebrows lifted, and he turned toward her, stretching a long arm along the back of the sofa between them. "You think you know?"

"Sure. Your brothers had done it. You were just carrying on the family tradition."

"Hey, my brothers just tried to do it," he corrected. "I succeeded."

Something in his voice alerted her to the truth, and she was surprised she hadn't seen it before. "It was important that you do better than they did."

He shrugged. "When you've got two big brothers—actually three counting my cousin Brendan—you're always coming along at the tag end of everything. They never let you forget that you're the runt of the litter. I wanted to rock the boat a little."

"Show people who you are," she suggested.

"Something like that." His lips curved in a smile. "Dad always had to go through the whole list of names before he got to me when I was in trouble. Gabriel-Brendan-Seth-Ryan, he'd yell."

"Is that why you want to go into arson investigation? To stand out from the rest of the Flanagan firefighters?"

He looked a little startled. "Maybe so, partly anyway. I guess I'm still looking for the thing that's just mine, no one else's."

He was confiding in her, and it felt surprisingly natural. "Maybe you've found it."

"I hope so." His fingertips brushed her shoulder. "What about you? What do you want beyond fixing up this place to sell and seeing Mandy through her surgery?"

Her mind went blank from the combination of the question and his nearness. She'd been so focused on her immediate aims that she hadn't really thought beyond them, except to envision a vague, happy future. What did she want?

The telephone rang, saving her from an answer she didn't know how to make.

"Excuse me." She picked up the receiver. "Hello." Her heart sank at the sound of her mother's high-pitched voice. "Hello, Mom. How are you? How is Dad?"

As usual, it was impossible to find out how her father really was. Her mother seemed to consider his emphysema a tedious excuse for not doing what she wanted him to do. And if she asked her father, of course he'd say he was fine because he didn't want to worry her.

Laura interrupted a long string of complaints about the retirement complex in which her parents lived in Arizona. "I have someone here right now, Mother. May I call you back later?"

Her mother switched gears immediately, getting abruptly to the reason for her call. Money. She persisted in believing that only selfishness kept her only daughter from funding her every whim.

"I'm sorry, Mom."

She turned away from Ryan. He was pretending interest in a magazine on the coffee table, but he'd have to be stupid not to realize something was going on.

"I wish I could help you, but I can't." She thought of her dwindling bank account with a moment of panic. "I'll call you back later. Goodbye." She hung up quickly, before she could say something she'd regret.

She stood staring down at the phone for a moment, not ready to face Ryan yet, aware that her palms were damp and her stomach churning.

He let the silence stretch for a few minutes before he spoke. "Family troubles?"

She took a breath. "You could say that."

He patted the couch next to him. "I bored you with mine. The least you can do is to return the favor."

She managed a smile as she sat down. "It's not much of a favor."

"Your parents are out in Arizona, I remember."

"For my father's health."

"Is he doing all right?"

"He's been better since they've been out there." She rubbed her forehead. "At least I think so. He always puts up such a good front when I talk to him that it's hard to be sure of that."

"You worry about him." His palm settled on the back of her neck, moving in slow, soothing circles. "Won't your mom level with you?"

How to explain her mother in a few well-chosen words? Impossible, but she had to say something.

"Mom seldom thinks of anything except as it affects her, I'm afraid. She sees my father's illness as a personal inconvenience." Her fingers were curling into a tight ball, and she deliberately relaxed them. "She's never stopped blaming Dad for selling their house here and moving into a smaller condo out there."

"I'm sorry." His tone was gentle. "I guess that kind of puts you in the middle."

The movement of his hand was easing the tension away. "There's always something. This time she wants me to put up the money so that they can move into a 'real house' instead of the condo." She shrugged. "I can't, obviously."

"Doesn't she understand that?"

"She's convinced that my husband couldn't possibly have left me as badly off as I say."

She stopped. She'd already said more than she intended. She wouldn't talk to Ryan about Jason.

It was Ryan's fault—for being here, for insisting on offering friendship, for making her long to confide in someone. She shook her head.

"Sorry. I shouldn't be unloading that on you."

"Hey, we're friends, aren't we?" He touched her chin lightly, tipping her face up so that she looked into his eyes. "Friends can level with each other."

"I guess so."

The words came out breathlessly. She wanted to tell him that she was fine, that she didn't need any help or anyone to lean on, but the words wouldn't seem to come. They got lost in the nearness of him.

The deep blue of Ryan's eyes seemed to grow even darker, more mysterious. His fingers stroked her cheek, warming where they touched.

She wanted to lean into his embrace and feel his arms close around her. Feel his lips on hers. He was going to kiss her—

Ryan pulled back, looking dazed and a little confused, as if he'd lost track of where he was and what he was doing.

"I—" He cleared his throat. "I guess I can see why you feel you have to stand on your own feet."

She struggled for composure, looking anywhere but at Ryan. "I have to. I can't count on them for any help, with Mandy or anything else."

They were talking about her parents. Not about them. Not about how Ryan had almost kissed her and then pulled away.

She glanced at the clock. "Well, it's getting late." He obviously regretted what had almost happened. She'd give him an excuse to leave.

"I guess so." He stood, and she could feel his relief. "Good night, Laura." In an instant he was gone.

Punching her pillow was doing absolutely nothing to help her get to sleep. Laura sat up in bed and wrapped her arms around her knees. The red numbers on the digital alarm clock informed her that it was nearly three in the morning.

She simply couldn't get those moments with Ryan out of her mind, no matter how she tried. She pressed her hand against her cheek, seeming to feel the warmth of his fingers. Denying the attraction she felt for him would be lying to herself, and she didn't do that.

All right, she was attracted to him. This feeling wasn't the hero worship she'd felt for him in high school. She wasn't even sure she believed in heroes any longer. But she was drawn inexorably to his easy smile and to the goodness she sensed behind it.

"A merry heart doeth good like a medicine." The scripture verse popped into her mind unbidden. It was probably something she'd learned in Siobhan Flanagan's church-school class, now that she thought about it. Ryan's mother had loved memorizing scripture, and she'd tried to pass that love along to a rambunctious group of early teens.

You never know when those words will come back to help you, she'd said.

What would Siobhan say now if she knew how far Laura had wandered from her teachings? She tried to push the thought away, but it clung. Siobhan would care—that she knew without thinking about it.

Siobhan and Laura's mother had been the same generation, living in the same town, attending the same church, but they'd been miles apart in temperament. Laura's throat tightened, remembering the emotional storms her mother had used to get her way, remembering the distress in her father's face whenever he tried to deal with them.

She would be a better role model than that for her daughter. She might not have the faith of someone like Siobhan, but she would do that.

She slipped out of bed and went barefoot across the

hall, easing open the door to Mandy's room. The night-light glowed softly, and the zebras and elephants kept watch. She tiptoed across the hooked rug.

Mandy lay on her side, teddy bear snuggled against her, one hand still on the puppy book. Laura smoothed the patchwork quilt over her—unnecessary, but she loved to feel the even rise and fall of Mandy's breathing.

Love choked her throat, fierce and protective. She had to make things right for Mandy. No matter who had let her down, she wouldn't let Mandy down. She bent to drop a feather-light kiss on her daughter's curls.

I'll make it right, my darling. I promise.

She went back to her own bedroom, still wired up and far from sleep. Once she'd have sought refuge in prayer or scripture at moments like this, but the barriers she'd put up between herself and God prevented that.

How could You let us down? Mandy is an innocent child. Where is Your help when we need it?

She rubbed her forehead. She shouldn't—

The outside lights came on, blazing through the windows that overlooked the alley, startling her into a throat-choked stillness.

She pressed her hand against her chest, feeling the thumping of her heart. Ridiculous, to be so upset because the lights had come on. Maybe it was Ryan's stray cat.

But he'd been kidding about that. He'd said so. He'd said they'd set the lights high enough that they wouldn't be triggered by something so low to the ground. Only by something larger. Like a man.

Heart in her throat, she crossed the room on tiptoe, as if someone outside could hear. She stopped at the window, stepping to the side so that she wouldn't cast a shadow on the shade. Carefully she eased the shade away from the window an inch so that she could look out.

The lights Ryan and Seth had installed illuminated the alleyway behind the house, casting every object into sharp relief. Nothing moved.

She leaned forward a little, scanning the area at the edge of the light. Was that something—a darker shadow within the shadows just beyond the circle of light? She held her breath, eyes straining to detect movement.

Nothing. She couldn't stand here all night, watching a shadow to see if it moved.

Steeling herself, she grasped the window frame and shoved. The window shrieked, resisting her. She forced it up and leaned out to look again.

The shadow she thought she'd seen was gone.

Ryan pushed open the glass door to the department headquarters building and then stopped. Lieutenant North was coming out, his face possibly even a little grimmer than it usually was.

"Flanagan." His curt nod substituted for a good morning. "Come on. It seems your girlfriend had an alarm in the night. She called in about it."

Ryan tried to speak evenly in spite of the fact that his heart was clenching. "She's not my girlfriend. Are they all right?" *Please, Father.*

North nodded, stopping at Ryan's car. Obviously he expected him to drive. Ryan unlocked the doors and slid in, turning the ignition key even before the other man was settled.

"What happened?" He tried, without success, to keep the tension out of his voice.

North snapped his seat belt. "She claims the motion lights in the alley went on around three in the morning. Says she thought she saw someone there. And she's found something she wants to show us."

"What?"

"She didn't say." North settled back with an abstracted frown.

Maybe it was just as well that the lieutenant didn't go in for idle chatter. His mind was spinning with images of the previous evening.

At least they'd put the lights up. Even if this turned out to be a false alarm, they'd taken that extra precautionary step. And Laura had been grateful, in spite of the fact that he'd had to talk her into letting them do it.

His fingers tightened on the steering wheel. After what he'd been able to read between the lines about her family, maybe he understood that fierce independence of hers a little better. The people in her life had let her down, and she was determined to stand on her own.

Still, she had begun to open up to him. Well, she had until he'd behaved like an idiot and let himself be distracted by the attraction he felt, instead of concentrating on what she needed.

Idiot. Jerk. Calling himself names didn't seem to

help. At least he hadn't kissed her. That was one small thing to congratulate himself for.

Seth had been right, little though he wanted to admit it. Laura didn't need romance in her life right now, not unless it was the real thing.

She needed a friend. Maybe, if he could keep his mind off his own reactions, he could be that.

He pulled up in front of Laura's building, tension riding his nerves. What had happened after he'd left last night?

She was obviously watching for them, because she opened the door quickly and ushered them inside.

"Back in the old kitchen." She led the way. "I don't want Mandy to realize something is wrong."

He glanced up the stairs, but all was quiet. Mandy, cocooned in her silent world, hadn't heard them.

"The outside lights came on around three this morning."

Laura was already talking as the door swung shut behind them. Probably she needed to go over the events a few times in order to wipe away the fear. He'd seen that in rookie firefighters after they'd gone through a bad experience. Each telling made the hard thing easier to take.

"But you didn't see anyone in the alley that you could identify?" North leaned against the counter, pulling out the omnipresent notebook.

"No." A shudder seemed to run through her.

Ryan had to resist the impulse to move closer to her. He was here on duty, not as a friend.

"Nothing moved in the light?" he probed.

She shook her head. "I thought I saw something or someone in the shadows at that end of the alley." She jerked a nod toward South Street. "When nothing moved, I opened the window. It took a minute or two, and by the time I leaned out and looked again, whatever I'd seen was gone."

"Gone?" North's tone was crisp. "Or never there?"

Laura's chin came up. "This morning I went out and checked. I found this."

She lifted a plastic trash bag to the scarred table. It clanked metallically as she set it down. She pulled the plastic away, and Ryan's nerves clenched. Inside the bag sat a battered can of paint thinner.

Chapter Six

Spring sunlight streamed through the stained-glass windows of Grace Church's children's wing. Laura went down the hall, her feet seeming to find the way by instinct. It had been years since she'd been in this building, but still, she knew the way to the kindergarten classroom.

Why had she come? She knew the answer, or at least the one she'd told herself this morning. She'd come because Ryan had been right—if she wanted to express her thanks to the church members who'd helped her, coming to the service was the way to do it.

Another reason lurked at the back of her mind, and it was one she had to force herself to acknowledge. She'd wanted to see a few friendly faces after that chilling experience two nights ago.

And after Lieutenant North's response to it. The arson investigator had promised increased police patrols. He'd taken the paint-thinner can for examination. But the whole time she'd been talking to him, she'd been overwhelmed with the conviction that he didn't believe a word she said.

Ryan might level with her about what his boss thought, if she had an opportunity to talk with him alone. Well, she'd make an opportunity. She and her child were the ones in danger. She had a right to know what was going on.

She paused outside the kindergarten classroom, peeking cautiously through the glass in the door. She hadn't wanted to leave Mandy in the Sunday school class without her, but Nolie had been there, eager to sign for Mandy. Somehow, quite without her knowing how, she'd been eased out of the room.

Now the group of four- and five-year-olds clustered in a circle around the teacher, heads bowed. Nolie's hands moved in the words of a prayer.

Laura's throat clenched. Mandy held hands with the children on either side of her. She looked content, as if she'd found a place where she belonged.

The prayer ended. Mandy looked up, saw her and ran toward the door, her face alight. Laura opened the door and stepped inside to catch her daughter in a hug.

"Did you have a good time?"

Mandy nodded, her hands flying in an attempt to tell everything they'd done. Nolie approached, smiling.

"She certainly did. She participated in every activity." She patted Mandy's head. "Why don't you get your papers and show your mommy?"

Mandy nodded and darted to the bulletin board where envelopes marked with each child's name held batches of church-school papers.

"This really went all right?"

Nolie smiled. "Perfectly. I hope you'll bring her again. I think this was a good experience for her."

It was an experience she hadn't provided for Mandy in the past. She'd wanted to protect her from the buffeting of children who wouldn't understand about her deafness. Maybe she'd been underestimating her small daughter.

Mandy shoved papers at her, her hands flying as she explained each of them. Then she smiled at Nolie and took her hand.

"I'll be teaching children's church today." Nolie patted her expanding waistline. "I told Gabe I'm getting in some mommy practice. Mandy would like to stay with me, if that's all right with you."

No! The instinctive response startled her. And made her feel ashamed, as well. She shouldn't hold Mandy back from doing something she wanted just because she wasn't used to being apart from her daughter.

"Fine." She managed a smile and gave Mandy a hug. "I'll see you after church, then."

When she reached the hallway, somehow she wasn't surprised to find Ryan waiting for her. The navy blazer, white shirt and red tie suited him, but made him seem almost like a stranger. She'd gotten used to the fireman's uniform that he wore like a second skin when he was on duty.

"How did it go?" He arched an eyebrow.

"Very well, I guess. Thanks to your sister-in-law." She turned somewhat reluctantly toward the sanctuary, and Ryan fell into step with her.

"Nolie's the best. Gabe is a lucky man."

A man that Ryan had no desire to emulate, apparently, at least when it came to settling down. She glanced at him, wondering what lay behind that easy smile. She'd learned a lot about Ryan in the past weeks—his friendliness, his persistence, his physical courage. But there was more to Ryan than the obvious.

They mounted the stairs, coming out into the long hallway lined with stained-glass windows that led to the sanctuary. She looked at the carved wooden door at the end of the hallway, and her steps slowed.

Ryan slanted a glance toward her. "What's up?"

"What do you mean?" He couldn't possibly guess her half-formed thoughts.

"If we go any slower, we'll be going backward. Don't you want to hear a sermon from my cousin? Or are you trying to get out of sitting with the Flanagans?"

"Neither." She shook her head. Okay, he did guess her thoughts. "I'm just a considerably different person from the teenager who used to be here every time the church doors were open. That's all."

Ryan came to a halt, propping one hand against the nearest window frame as if prepared to stay there all day. "Why is that?"

Annoyance flickered through her. "I'm not sure that's any of your business."

If she'd hoped to make him angry, she didn't succeed. His interested expression didn't change.

"Maybe not. But I'd still like to know what you've got against God."

His perception took her breath away. Or maybe she was a lot more obvious than she'd thought.

"Do you really have to ask that question?" She looked at the rose and green glass of the window, hoping to hide the tears that filled her eyes.

Ryan's hand brushed hers. "I don't know why Mandy was born deaf. I don't know the why of a lot of bad things, but that doesn't mean God's to blame."

She fought to hold the words back, but they spilled out anyway. "I asked Him for help when I was desperate. Over and over again. He never answered." She shook her head angrily, cutting off any answer he might make. "Forget it. You don't have answers. No one does. We'd better get inside before the service starts."

She whirled toward the door, eager to get away from Ryan and that embarrassing moment of self-revelation. Ryan reached around her to grasp the handle. He held it for a moment, so that she was forced to wait.

"You're probably right," he said slowly. "I don't have answers. But I know what my mother would say to that question. She'd say that other people are God's hands on earth."

He yanked the door open and ushered her through before she could think of a response.

Laura still hadn't found an answer to the questions Ryan's comment had raised as she followed his car down a country road after the service. She tried to stow the thoughts away for later consideration. She had more pressing things on her mind now.

Ryan had seemed surprised when she'd accepted

his invitation to Nolie and Gabe's farm after church. As he'd told her, the Flanagan family got together en masse every Sunday for dinner, and when the weather was nice, they went to the farm.

She wasn't really interested in the farm or in the puppies Ryan had promised to show Mandy. What she wanted was to corner Ryan long enough to find out what was happening with the investigation.

She looked in the rearview mirror. Mandy sat quietly, absorbed in coloring the papers she'd brought from church school. At the moment she was carefully filling in purple flowers around an image of Jesus and the children, her little face intent.

She'd done that at Mandy's age, she remembered, saving all the pictures and papers so that she could play Sunday school at home with her dolls. Something seemed to twist in her stomach. This was the first time Mandy had been to Sunday school. She'd evaded the subject of her daughter's spiritual development, letting her own feelings interfere.

She could take Mandy back to Grace Church, of course. But doing so meant confronting her own feelings, and she didn't think she was ready to do that.

Why, God? Why haven't You helped me? The familiar refrain began in her mind, but it was interrupted this time by Ryan's words. *My mother would say...that other people are God's hands on earth.*

The words pressed against her, demanding attention. She shook her head, as if to shake them away.

Mandy looked up at the movement, her dark-brown eyes reflected in the mirror. Laura smiled at her.

"We're almost there. Look, Ryan is turning in." Even when she couldn't sign, she talked to Mandy, hoping some understanding came through.

Mandy leaned forward to look out the window, gazing entranced at the colorful sign on the gatepost. Nolie's Ark, it said, and a variety of smiling animals poked their heads out of the painted ark.

Laura pulled up next to Ryan's car under the branches of an oak tree that was just leafing out. As she slid from the car, Ryan was already there, helping Mandy out of the back seat.

Mandy tugged at Ryan's hand impatiently. "Dog," she said carefully.

Ryan blinked, glancing at Laura. "I've never heard her talk before."

"She doesn't very often, but sometimes she tries. She'd started to talk before her hearing worsened, so that gave her a head start. It's good for her to verbalize." She ruffled Mandy's curls. "Good talking, sweetheart."

"Dogs it is," Ryan said, and she thought his heartiness covered emotion he didn't want to show. "I happen to know there are puppies in the barn."

Laura glanced toward the picnic tables, where what seemed a horde of Flanagans already milled around, putting out food. "Shouldn't we go and speak to your family first? I ought to help."

He clasped Mandy's hand, swinging it. "Helping can wait. We've got puppies to see first."

Mandy grabbed her hand. "Puppies," she said.

Hearing her daughter verbalize again overcame any compunction she might feel. "Right. Puppies."

Ryan led them across the lawn toward a red wooden barn. "Relax. Everyone understands, and they don't expect you to help. Just to enjoy."

"They're nice to include us."

Nolie came out a screened door at the side of the white farmhouse just then, carrying a tray. Gabe immediately took it from her. He bent to drop a kiss on her cheek and a quick, gentle pat on her rounded stomach. Nolie glanced their way and waved.

Laura waved back, her throat tightening.

"Sickening, isn't it?" Ryan grinned. "They've been married for nearly a year and they still act like newlyweds."

"They're obviously very happy."

She thought of what Nolie had said about Gabe's reaction to having a daughter. Had Jason ever been that happy about her pregnancy? He'd wanted a son. Maybe—

She cut that thought off ruthlessly. She would never let herself think that their lives might have been different if Mandy had been a boy. Or if Mandy had been born hearing.

Mandy was perfect. If Jason hadn't been able to see that, it was his misfortune.

Mandy, running ahead of them, stopped, staring into the white-fenced paddock, her eyes huge and round. Ryan grinned, lifting her so that she could see over the fence a little better.

"Those are miniature horses, Mandy." He glanced at Nolie. "Maybe you'd better translate. I don't think my signing extends far enough for that."

A gray donkey came to lean its head over the rail fence, looking at them inquiringly. Ryan patted its soft ears and guided Mandy's hand to stroke them.

"His name is Toby. He likes boys and girls." He ran his hand down the donkey's back. "See the way there's a cross in his fur? People say that's because a donkey carried Jesus on Palm Sunday."

Her throat clenched as she signed the words. Ryan's words were another reminder of all that was missing in her daughter's life. Obviously they couldn't be around the Flanagan family without constant reminders of the faith they lived.

She cleared her throat. "Are you sure the mama dog isn't going to mind our looking at her puppies?"

"No, Missy's a sweet dog. She loves people. One of many strays Nolie has rescued. Missy was originally intended to be trained as a service dog, but she's turned into a family pet instead."

"That's what Nolie does—trains service animals?"

Ryan pushed back the sliding door on the barn, nodding. "She trains the animals, and she also works with people who have disabilities. That's how Gabe met her. He had to get a seizure alert dog after he was hurt in a fire."

He said the words so matter-of-factly, but this had to be an emotional subject for Ryan. His brother and father had both suffered injuries on the job, but everyone said when it came to fighting fire, Ryan had no fear. She'd seen that for herself, and she didn't begin to understand it.

"Hey, Missy." A black-and-white border collie came to meet them, her plumed tail waving gently. "I brought someone to see your babies."

There was a scrabble of feet on the rough-planked barn floor, and six black-and-white puppies romped toward them. Mandy squealed with delight and darted past Ryan.

"Puppies," she said again, reaching out her arms toward them.

Laura's throat went tight. "That's the most she's ever verbalized in such a short period of time."

"She's had a lot of stimulation today," Ryan said, ruffling a puppy's fur. "Maybe it's good for her."

There didn't seem to be any criticism in his words—just a simple observation. It shouldn't make her feel guilty, but it did.

"I just want to keep her safe."

"I know." He snapped his fingers to the dog. "Come on, Missy. "Let's take your puppies out in the sunshine."

The dog seemed to understand him. She ambled through the barn door and onto the grass, the puppies tumbling behind her. Mandy trotted along, beaming, and dropped to the grass, hauling the nearest puppy into her lap.

Laura opened her mouth to protest the probable grass stains on Mandy's red-and-white dress, but closed it again. Her daughter's happiness was too important to let a few grass stains get in the way.

Ryan carried what looked like a saddle blanket from the barn and spread it on the grass. "I'm not guaranteeing how clean this thing is, but have a seat if you're willing to risk it."

"It's fine." She sat down, the soft skirt she'd worn for church folding around her.

Ryan collapsed on the blanket next to her, smiling as one of the puppies climbed onto his lap. "Cute little things, aren't they?" He tickled under its chin. "Nolie's trying to find homes for them, you know. They're about ready to leave their mama."

"Oh, no. The last thing I need is a puppy to take care of."

He plopped the puppy in her lap, and her hands curved around it instinctively.

"It'd make a good watch dog."

She lifted her eyebrows, distracted by the puppy licking her fingers. "It's the size of your hand. I don't think it would provide much protection."

"He'll grow." He ruffled the puppy's fur, his fingers brushing hers. "He's already big enough to make noise if he hears something unusual. That could be a good thing."

"The lights are protection enough."

Mandy tried to pick up two puppies at once and then, giggling, toppled toward Ryan. He caught her easily, his big hands gentle, and gave her a hug. They both looked at her, both smiling.

Laura's heart lurched. Anyone looking at the three of them might see think they were seeing a happy family. It almost felt that way.

It shouldn't. Something approaching panic brushed her heart. That was a dangerous thing to think, because she might actually start to believe it was possible.

Laura leaned on the paddock fence next to Siobhan later that afternoon, watching as Ryan led the donkey at a gentle walk with two giggling girls on its back. Mandy had changed into a pair of jeans and a T-shirt belonging to Ryan's niece, Shawna, and somehow that act had made the two girls inseparable.

Ryan waved at her. "You're next," he said.

"I'm too big to ride a donkey. Thanks anyway."

"That won't be the end of it," Siobhan said. "I've never seen anyone like Ryan for persuading people to do things they don't want to do."

"He's not getting me on a donkey, no matter how persuasive he is." Although Siobhan was probably right about Ryan's skills—he'd talked Mandy onto the donkey in spite of her tendency to cling to his neck.

Siobhan smiled. "He's so good with children. He should have a houseful of his own."

She wasn't going to touch that comment with a ten-foot pole. "I appreciate the effort he's making with Mandy. She's enjoying herself so much."

Mandy looked like any little girl, enjoying a donkey ride with a friend. Her arms were around Shawna's waist, and they wore identical grins.

Laura's heart twisted. That was what she wanted for her child—that normalcy that others took for granted.

"She certainly got along very well in church school today," Siobhan said. "Have you thought about putting her in pre-school a few hours a week? The one where our grandkids go is excellent."

She wasn't going to expose Mandy to the rough and tumble of pre-school, no matter how excellent.

"Not just now. She's probably going to have her

cochlear implant in the next month or so, and I'd like to get her through that first."

"I understand. That's a big enough thing to deal with now." Siobhan's hand closed warmly over hers. "I'm praying for her. And for you."

Her throat tightened. There was only one response to that. "Thank you."

Ryan led the donkey to the fence next to them. "Okay, girls, that's it for you. It's Laura's turn to ride the donkey now."

"Not a chance," she said quickly. "I'm not dressed for riding."

"Excuses, excuses." He patted the donkey's back. "All you have to do is sit there."

Siobhan laughed. "I'll leave you to it. Come on, girls, let's go get some lemonade and cookies." She held out her hands, and the two girls scampered under the fence and grabbed them.

Mandy went off without a backward glance. She seemed to know instinctively that Siobhan was some-one she could trust, and to understand her without the need for signing.

"Come on." Ryan caught her hand. "I'll lead the donkey, I promise."

"Listen, just because you're a big brave fireman doesn't mean other people have your courage. I don't want to ride him. It's too far off the ground."

Something flickered in Ryan's eyes. "It doesn't take courage to do something you're not afraid of."

For a moment she could only stare at him. "But— how could you not be afraid of a fire?" She relived, only too vividly, the terror she'd felt when she'd woken to the blare of the smoke alarm.

He shrugged, his gaze fixed on their hands, clasped atop the rough rail of the fence. "I don't know. Adrenaline takes over, I guess. I've always been that way about any physical challenge—give me a cliff to climb or a roof to jump off, and I'm your man."

Ryan was giving her a window into his soul that she suspected he didn't open for many people.

"Is that a good thing?"

"I used to think so. Now, I'm not so sure."

She'd thought she didn't understand what made him tick. Now he was showing her. Trusting her with it.

"What changed that for you?" she asked carefully.

His fingers moved restlessly against hers. "You know my father had a heart attack on the job."

She nodded. Had that been what made him realize his own mortality?

"You probably don't know it was my fault." His voice sounded even, but she could hear the pain in it. That pain grasped her heart and wouldn't let go.

"How could it be? Ryan—"

"I was first in. I outran my support. Got trapped. My father was trying to get to me when he collapsed."

She clasped his hand, immeasurably moved by his confiding in her, longing to help and not sure how to do it. "I'm sure he didn't blame you."

"I blamed myself. Maybe I shouldn't be in a job where I can endanger other people."

Saying the right thing seemed impossible. "Is that the real reason why you want to join the arson team?"

He shrugged. "At least I don't put someone else in danger when I'm using my brains." His smile flickered. "Not that North thinks I'm overly endowed in that department."

"He looks like the kind of person who doesn't think highly of anyone." This seemed to be her opportunity to ask about the investigation, but she hesitated.

"North is chronically suspicious, that's for sure. He even—"

He stopped, but she thought she knew what he'd been going to say.

"He's suspicious of me. Is that what you mean?"

Ryan seemed to draw back, even though he didn't move. "There's no reason to suspect you," he said.

A chill went down her spine at his careful choice of words. "But he does. Why on earth would he think that? Did he find something in the investigation that points to me?"

Ryan's eyes met hers. "Don't ask me that, Laura. I can't talk to you about the investigation."

There was a finality to his tone that shook her—a cool professionalism that seemed to turn him from her friend into someone else entirely. The man who'd confided in her was gone, replaced by someone she didn't know.

"I see." She pulled her hand away from his.

"I'm sorry." He had the grace to look miserable about it. "It's my job."

"I know." She tried to muster a smile, but she couldn't quite manage.

It was his job. She'd seen that single-minded determination in him before, when he'd disregarded her protests and snatched Mandy from her when he'd rescued them from the fire.

She'd learned more than she'd expected about Ryan today, but she wasn't sure it was what she'd wanted to know. For all his friendliness and charm, all the caring he'd shown her and Mandy, Ryan would put his job before other people.

Before her.

Chapter Seven

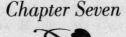

He just plain wasn't good at this personal relationship stuff, Ryan decided. He helped Jerry White unload the plastering supplies in front of Laura's house a couple of nights after the Sunday picnic that had started so well and ended so badly.

"Good thing you showed up to lend a hand, buddy," Jerry grumbled. "I was already up to my eyeballs without this extra job."

"You're just lucky anyone trusts you enough to do their plastering. If they knew you like I do—"

Jerry slammed the door of the panel truck and elbowed him. "So, is this woman the latest girlfriend?"

"Just an old friend. That's all." At least that's what he intended. After the way they'd parted on Sunday, maybe even friendship wasn't on Laura's agenda.

What did Laura expect—that he'd destroy his chances at the job he wanted just to make sure she felt better? It wasn't as if knowing what Garrett North was up to would actually allay her fears.

As far as he could tell, the man suspected anyone and everyone, including Laura. The only thing he knew for sure was that a bulldog like North wouldn't give up until he found out who'd started that fire.

Nor would he. He headed for Laura's front door in Jerry's wake. That was his job, and he'd do it, no matter who got in the way.

Still, coming to help with the plastering was his way of trying to make peace with Laura. He wouldn't give up on their friendship as easily as she seemed prepared to.

But he wouldn't let their relationship get any closer than friendship. He was just plain no good at the emotional stuff. He'd treat Laura the way he would any other friend, like Jerry, for instance. He grinned. Laura, with her slim figure, creamy skin and that riot of dark hair falling to her shoulders, wasn't remotely like Jerry.

Laura swung the door open and gave him a rather wary look. "Ryan." She smiled at Jerry and held out her hand. "And you must be Jerry. Thank you so much for coming. You're a real lifesaver."

Jerry stumbled over his own feet. "Sure, no problem. Glad to do it."

Right. Ryan gave his erstwhile buddy a shove. "Let's get moving, Jerry. This stuff is heavy."

Laura's eyebrows lifted. "Are you planning to help with the plastering?"

"Sure thing." He scanned the jeans and sweatshirt she wore. "You?"

"Since Jerry's fitting my job in as a favor, of course I'm going to help." She turned and started up the stairs. "Come this way."

Jerry doing it as a favor? Only because he'd pushed him into it.

He shot Jerry a disgusted look, and Jerry grinned back, clearly not a bit sorry. They jostled each other as they started up the stairs.

They came out into the big open room at the top of the stairs. Laura had put all the lights on, making the space even more desolate.

"I know it doesn't look like much." She seemed to be reading their thoughts. "But once the plaster is repaired and I can paint the walls, it will make a huge difference. The woodwork is in good shape, and so is that beautiful pressed-tin ceiling."

Jerry was looking around with a professional eye. "This is really not too bad. With the three of us working, we ought to make good headway." He gave Laura a smile that set Ryan's teeth on edge.

"What about this wall?" He tapped the nearby partition that split the room awkwardly. "Didn't you tell me it's coming down?"

"Right." Laura sketched an opening with her hand. "My buyer wants this space open and light. She plans to open a vintage clothing store in the downstairs, and this will be her workroom."

"Well, let's give her what she wants," Jerry said. "Ryan, how about if you haul some water."

He might have known Jerry would give him the donkey work. Still, if carrying water got the room finished and Jerry out of here, that would be worth it. He grabbed a couple of buckets and headed for the sink.

Some of his irritation ebbed away as they worked.

No matter how much of a clown Jerry had been in high school, he seemed to know his stuff. He and Laura were soon well-covered in plaster as they tried to master getting the stuff onto the wall instead of themselves. Jerry just kept whistling away, the smooth strokes of his trowel turning dismal into pristine.

"Okay, buddy, I have to admit it." Ryan stopped for a moment's rest, admiring the swath of smooth plaster. "You actually do know what you're doing."

"Hey, my dad insisted I had to live up to his standards. Just like you and your dad."

"Maybe so." His father wasn't totally reconciled to the idea of the arson squad, but at least he wasn't openly hostile to it.

It's not as if Ryan wants to become a plumber, Seth had pointed out when things got noisy.

"Yeah, who would believe when we were back in high school that we'd actually turn into responsible citizens?" Jerry grinned at Laura. "That guy was the worst." He jerked his head toward Ryan. "Talk about taking stupid chances!"

"I seem to remember that about him." If Laura was thinking about what he'd been foolish enough to confide in her, she didn't show it. "But he always seemed to land on his feet, like a cat with nine lives."

"Would you mind not talking about me as if I weren't here?" Ryan asked plaintively. "I do have feelings, you know."

Jerry hooted at that. "Put your feelings on hold and get back to work, buddy. We've got a wall to finish."

Surprisingly enough, they did finish. Laura looked

about ready to collapse by the time the final section was done, and Ryan wasn't far behind. Jerry, on the other hand, looked perfectly ready to go on and plaster another acre or two of wall. Still whistling, he picked up two buckets and headed for the stairs.

When Laura started to pick up an armload of equipment to carry down, Ryan caught her arm. Her skin warmed under his fingers, and he had to remind himself again. A friend. Just a friend.

"Forget about that stuff. Jerry and I will load everything. I'm sure you want to check on Mandy and sink into a hot tub."

Laura raised those dark level brows. "Are you implying I'm dirty?"

"Only about as bad as I am." He grinned. "Go on. We'll take care of the clean-up."

He thought she'd argue, but she just nodded.

He turned toward the steps and then stopped when she touched his arm in turn.

"Do you have a minute? There's something I want to ask you."

More questions about the investigation? If so, she was going to be angry with him all over again.

"Sure. What?"

"Will you forgive me?"

That startled him. "For what?"

"You know." Her dark eyes were very serious. "I was wrong to try and pump you about the case. And wrong to get upset when you couldn't answer me. You're just doing your job."

The tension inside him eased, making him realize

how much the breach between them had bothered him. "Forget it. Look, we both know how awkward this situation is. If I could tell you anything, I would. You know that."

"Yes." There was something reserved about her smile that he didn't quite understand. "You and your family have been good friends."

Now it was his turn to raise his eyebrows. "You make that sound like it's in the past. We plan to go on being good friends, if you'll let us."

"Of course."

"In that case, I'll be back Thursday to help with the painting. It's my day off."

For an instant he thought she'd make an excuse to put him off. Then she nodded.

She was agreeing, wasn't she? Still, he could sense something held back.

He hesitated. He could press her. But if he did, he'd be violating his own promise to himself. Be a friend, but stay out of emotional territory.

That was what was best for both of them. He knew that. So why did it feel so wrong to accept her agreement at face value and turn away?

Stomach churning, Laura turned the ignition one more time, to be greeted by a click and relentless silence. Why now, of all times?

A tap on the car window made her turn. Ryan stood there, looking ready to work in faded jeans and a polo shirt. She opened the door.

"Your battery is dead."

"Thanks, but I already figured that out." She slid out, fumbling in her bag for her cell phone. "I'll have to call a cab. I'm sorry I didn't let you know not to come, but something came up at the last minute."

He opened the rear door, helping Mandy out and responding to her smile and hug.

"You don't have to call a cab. You can take my car." He fished the keys from his pocket and held them out to her.

It would be yet another favor she owed him. "Then you'll be stuck here."

"I can get on with the painting."

The man had an answer for everything. "I don't think—" She stopped, realizing that Mandy was tugging at her sleeve. "What is it, honey?"

Mandy's hands flew, and then she attached herself to Ryan's pant leg.

He grinned. "Even I could figure that one out. Sure, I'll be glad to drive you."

She looked, exasperated, from one smiling face to the other. "You don't even know where we're going."

"Doesn't matter. I have all day." He took Mandy's hand and led her to his car, parked behind hers. "Do you want me to move her booster seat?"

She glanced at her watch. She'd wasted too much time already, trying to get her bucket of bolts to cooperate. "I'll get it."

In the few minutes it took to move the booster seat and get Mandy settled, she'd given herself a short lecture on attitude. She should be glad Ryan had shown up. He was just being a friend, and she had too few of those to scare one away.

"Thanks." She slid into the passenger seat of his car and buckled her seat belt. "That clunker of mine has a way of dying at the worst times."

"It's no problem." Ryan started the car. "Where are we going?"

"The hospital. Dr. Marsh's office called, and they had a cancellation. He can see Mandy this morning."

"That *is* good news." He glanced at the back seat. Mandy was engrossed in the book she'd brought. The puppy book, of course. She'd been obsessed with it since that visit to the farm. "Does she understand what's going on?"

"A little. I've tried to explain the whole thing to her, but since her hearing has gotten so much worse, I'm afraid she's forgotten what it's like to hear much of anything."

"Why does she wear the hearing aids, then? I mean, if they don't really help?"

"Her therapist recommended using them, just in case she's picking up some sounds. And it keeps her used to having something on her ear, so that it'll be easier when she has the implant."

He nodded. "I remember seeing a picture of a child wearing one. The part that shows is the microphone, right?"

"How did you know that?" Most people didn't.

"Looked it up on the Internet." He grinned. "It's amazing what you can find. I actually now know enough not to embarrass myself when you talk about the implant."

For a moment she couldn't speak. Ryan barely knew them, and he'd gone to the trouble of researching Mandy's problems. It contrasted so sharply with Jason's reaction when he'd learned that their daughter was deaf.

"That was thoughtful of you." She had to clear her throat because her voice had gone husky.

"I'm interested. So, if all goes well today, do you think they'll get the procedure on the calendar soon?"

"I hope so." A shiver went down her spine. *Soon.* She had to get the house finished, because if she didn't succeed with the sale—

No, she wasn't going to think that. It would work out. It had to.

"It's going to be okay." Ryan seemed to be reading her thoughts again. "I have a good feeling about it. Your buyer is going to love what you've done."

"I keep telling myself everything will go the way I want." She glanced in the rearview mirror. "This procedure is Mandy's best chance at a hearing life. I can't let anything interfere with her getting the implant."

"And then what happens?" Ryan kept his eyes on the road. "You won't leave Suffolk, will you?"

"I'd like to stay here," she said carefully. Don't read too much into it, she told herself. He's asking as a friend, that's all. "Mandy will need therapy for a while to learn to make best use of the implant, and this is a good place for her to get it."

"So you'll stay."

"I'll still have to find another place to live. And a part-time job." Even if she got the price she expected for the building, her finances would be tight for some time.

"It'll happen." He·reached across to pat her hand. "You'll see. Suffolk is a good place to live, and you have friends here."

Friends, including Ryan. The hospital came into view ahead of them, and she couldn't help the involuntary way her hand clasped his.

"It's going to be okay," he repeated, and squeezed her hand.

They were simple words. The kind of words she used to reassure Mandy when things went wrong. Every mother said that, probably.

She just hadn't realized how much she'd longed to hear them herself. Longed to have someone tell her things were going to be all right.

Tears stung her eyes, and she blinked them back quickly. She took pride in standing on her own. She did.

But she couldn't deny how good it felt to have someone with her. Someone who understood and cared, even as a friend.

She looked at that thought, appalled at what it implied. She'd been telling herself that she didn't want anything from Ryan except friendship. She'd actually begun to believe it.

But turning into the hospital lot, knowing that soon she'd confront the possibility that Mandy's implant would be a reality, she longed for more.

She took a deep breath. It doesn't matter what you want. Ryan is offering friendship, nothing else.

That was true. She knew it.

Unfortunately she also knew she ought to admit another truth to herself, even if she never told Ryan. Her feelings for him had already gone beyond friendship, and there was nothing she could do about that.

Was there anything worse than sitting in a hospital waiting room? Ryan tried not to fidget. This room wasn't like the emergency room where he'd waited more than once for news about another firefighter. People sat here for ordinary appointments, not life-threatening emergencies.

But lives would still be changed by what was going on in the exam room where Dr. Marsh examined Mandy and Laura waited for his verdict. If he'd had the right to go in with them, maybe he could have helped.

No. That was a stupid idea. He didn't have the kind of relationship with Laura that would permit that. Even if he did, she might still have wanted to go in alone. That fierce determination to have the best for her child didn't even let her see anyone else just now.

The tiger-like ferocity of her love was more than a little scary to someone like him. Face it, he'd gotten through life on a combination of charm and physical prowess. He'd always thought that was plenty for anyone.

But neither of those qualities was of much use to Laura and Mandy right now.

He propelled himself out of the brown plastic chair and paced across the room. The rack next to the receptionist's desk had an assortment of pamphlets, some on cochlear implants. He snatched a few and stalked back to his chair.

He'd managed to hold up his end of a short conversation, thanks to his Internet research, but it sure wouldn't hurt to know a little more about something that was so important to Laura and Mandy. He owed them that, as a friend.

They came out, and he stuffed the pamphlets into his pocket and went to meet them.

"So, how'd it go?"

Mandy held up a coloring book that showed a child in a hospital bed. She pulled a green lollipop out of her mouth. She smiled, showing him a green tongue.

"It looks as if Mandy liked Dr. Marsh. How about you?"

He could feel Laura's tension without touching her, and his nerves sprang to attention. If the appointment had gone badly—

"He says Mandy is an excellent candidate for the procedure." Tears filled Laura's eyes, and she dashed them away with the back of her hand. "It's stupid to cry about it when I'm happy."

He caught her hand. "It seems like a pretty good reason to me."

She gave him a watery smile. "I guess. Why don't we get out of here?"

When they were in the car, she began giving him a blow by blow account of everything Marsh had said and done. He wasn't dumb enough to think that made him anyone special. He was just there, and she needed to talk. He drove and listened until she finally seemed to run down.

"When does he think he'll do the procedure?" he prompted.

He glanced into the rearview mirror as he turned into Laura's street. Mandy caught his gaze and smiled, as if to share some secret happiness. A ridiculous warmth swept through him.

"Ten days. If all the tests go well, they'll schedule the surgery in ten days."

"That sounds like disbelief in your voice."

She pushed a strand of curly dark hair behind her ear in a gesture he'd seen often. "I guess it is. I've been driving toward this for so long without thinking about anything else. Now that it's almost here, I don't know what to feel."

"Elation? Apprehension?" He'd probably feel both of those if Mandy were his daughter. Maybe he did anyway.

"Both." Her lips curved. "Add in some plain old fear, and you're on the right track."

He reached across to catch her hand and squeeze it. "She'll be all right. You said yourself that Dr. Marsh is the best person for the job. And in just eleven days the procedure will be over and you'll be celebrating."

"Well, I might save the celebration for another month. Mandy has to heal from the surgery before they activate the implant. Probably a month, he said."

"That's not long to wait."

"No." Her breath caught in an audible gasp. "I've got to get the house done. The hospital requires a deposit in advance from people who don't have insurance."

"You'll be done. Look how far you've come already." He drew up to the building. "I have the rest of the day free, so I'll help with the painting."

Laura looked as if she'd stopped listening. Instead she was looking at a white paper that fluttered from a piece of tape on her front door. Apprehension darkened her eyes.

"Now what?"

He slid out. "I'll get Mandy. Go ahead and see what that is."

Nothing, probably. How important could it be? But a chill seemed to brush his skin. Laura had had too many little things going wrong lately.

When he and Mandy reached her, she was crumpling the paper in her hand. She looked as if she'd like to do the same to whoever had written it.

"What's going on?"

She shoved the paper at him, as if inviting him to read it, and turned to unlock the door. "Honestly, I think that committee is on a power binge. What will they want me to add next—an original nineteenth-century outhouse?"

He smoothed the note out. Bradley Potter. He should have known.

"Well, that complaint is just ridiculous. How do they expect security lights to 'blend in to the existing ambience' of the structure? They didn't have security lights then."

"Don't ask me." She pushed her hair back in a weary gesture. "Every day it seems Potter's handing me a request for something else, and I don't have the time or money to fight them."

He felt a sharp spurt of annoyance toward Brad Potter. "Well, look, don't worry about this one. I think I can probably rig the lights so that the shutters hide the mechanism. They can't ask for more than that. You have a right to be safe, whether it's historically accurate or not. If the committee doesn't agree, I'll bring the fire department down on them."

"You shouldn't have to work on those lights again. You've done enough. I can—"

"I'll do it. I have all day, remember?"

His cell phone picked that moment to ring. He yanked it out of his pocket impatiently. "Flanagan."

The voice at the other end was North's. He turned away slightly so that Laura couldn't read his expression.

"I'll be right there." He snapped it off.

"What is it? What's happened?" Laura's face had paled.

Obviously he hadn't done a very good job of hiding what he felt. He may as well tell her—it was probably all over the news already anyway.

"That was North. There's been another arson attempt, two blocks over."

"Was anyone—"

"No," he said quickly. "Apparently the fire fizzled out. They didn't even discover the damage until an hour ago, and it must have been started during the night."

"Another one, that close." Her brown eyes were huge and dark.

He clasped her hands in a quick, hard grip. "Look,

this might be good news. The guy's made a mistake, and that might lead us to him."

"Right." She took a breath, obviously trying for control. "You have to go. Thanks for this morning."

"I'm glad I was here. And please, don't worry about those lights. I'll do them as soon as I can."

He bent to give Mandy a quick hug. He straightened, wishing he could do the same to Laura.

But he shouldn't. He turned and went quickly to the car before he could give in to the impulse.

Chapter Eight

Supper was over, Mandy in her pajamas, and still she hadn't heard anything from Ryan. Laura leaned against the window, hand pressed on the smooth pane, looking down at the street. Nothing. He hadn't come, he hadn't called.

Well, Ryan didn't have to report in to her. They didn't have that sort of relationship.

Evading the question of what sort of relationship they did have, she turned to Mandy. "How about watching a video before bedtime?" she signed.

Mandy nodded and ran to the video cabinet to pull out her favorite and slide it into the machine. Laura had to smile at her absorbed expression as the familiar story started. Videos didn't take the place of an old-fashioned bedtime story, but they did have their uses.

She realized she was starting toward the window again and turned away, busying herself with picking up the newspaper she'd left on the floor. The morning paper hadn't had a story about the latest fire, but she'd watched a brief report on the television news.

It hadn't given her much information she didn't already have from Ryan, but the images of the scorched porch had chilled her with their reminders. The owners of that building had been fortunate, though. The fire had gone out quickly, doing little but cosmetic damage.

The television reporter had speculated, of course, about the possibility of a firebug in their midst. If there was a pyromaniac on the loose, it was odd that he'd failed so badly in this effort. Perhaps someone or something had frightened him away before he could be sure the fire caught.

Her pacing had taken her to the window that overlooked the alley. And the lights. The note from Bradley Potter lay on the table, seeming to look at her accusingly.

A wave of restlessness went through her. Ryan had said he'd fix the lights, but he hadn't come. What if someone from the historical preservation committee happened by tonight and saw that she hadn't heeded their warning?

Logic said the committee would hardly expect her to have fixed the problem in a single day, but she was driven by something stronger than logic.

Ten days until Mandy's surgery. She couldn't afford to be held up endlessly by the preservation committee. Even if Ryan was right about the power of the fire-safety regulations against the preservation committee, that could take time. She couldn't risk delay.

Mandy was snuggled up on the sofa, already half

asleep. She tucked the afghan over her and put the monitor next to her pillow.

"I have to go out back and do some work, sweetheart. Just tap the monitor if you want me, okay?" They'd rigged up the method of signaling when she'd realized Mandy was old enough to have her mother a few rooms away at times.

Mandy nodded, staring past her mother to the screen. Laura bent to drop a kiss on her cheek and then hurried down the stairs. She switched on lights as she went. It was already dusk. If she were going to rig up something to hide the light fixtures, she'd have to do it now.

Leaving the back door ajar, she put the monitor on the window ledge. Strains of music from the video floated through it, nothing else. Mandy was only a flight of stairs away, she reminded herself.

She looked up at the lights, seeing what Ryan had meant about the shutters. They could be pulled out to hide the fixture without covering the electronic eye that detected movement. She ought to be able to do a temporary fix, leaving a more permanent solution until later.

The long aluminum ladder still lay in the back hallway where Seth and Ryan had left it. She manhandled the ladder out the door and up, surprised by its weight. The ladder swayed a bit before slithering into place against the house.

Okay, she could do this. It wouldn't even require tools to pull the shutters out. She grasped the ladder, shaking it to be sure it was stable as she'd seen her father do hundreds of times.

Somewhere in the back of her mind a caution sounded, but she ignored it. A few minutes and she'd be done. She started up the metal rungs.

She'd been climbing ladders since she was a kid. This was nothing. Halfway up, she glanced down at the concrete alley. Well, it wouldn't be a pleasant fall, but she didn't intend to fall.

Finally high enough, she reached out. The shutter was just beyond her fingertips. She should have set up the ladder closer to the window, but she could manage. Grasping the ladder with her left hand, she reached out with her right, straining toward the shutter.

The ladder shuddered. It swayed. A spasm of fear clutched her stomach. She braced her hand against the brick wall, fingers scrabbling to find something to hang on to.

Nothing. She couldn't hold it, it was going to fall—

"Laura!" The fear in Ryan's shout echoed hers.

She didn't dare move to look down, but she knew he was there, grabbing the ladder, steadying it, slamming it into place with the strength of his body.

"Get down. Now." His voice grated in a way she'd never heard before.

She was too grateful to take offense. Clutching the cold aluminum with both hands, she slithered her way down the ladder. Her legs shook, and she seemed to have left her stomach up there someplace, but she was all right.

She slid the last few rungs and felt Ryan's hands grab her firmly, almost angrily.

"Are you crazy?"

He was shaking. Ryan forced himself to push down the emotions that raged through him. He wanted to shake Laura silly for scaring him that way. Or kiss her senseless.

Fortunately he had just enough control to know that neither of those were good options. Still, he couldn't quite hold his voice steady.

"Are you *trying* to hurt yourself? That aluminum ladder is dangerous. *I* wouldn't go up it without someone steadying it, and there you were—"

He stopped. He was wrong. He didn't have enough control to keep his hands off her. He backed up a step.

Laura had sense enough to look embarrassed. "I thought I could go up and do a temporary fix on the lights. Just in case someone from the historical preservation committee came by tonight."

That brought his anger bubbling again. "I told you I'd take care of it."

Her stubborn chin firmed. "It's not your problem. It's mine."

He was actually grinding his teeth in frustration. "Will you please listen to yourself? You're being irrational. The committee certainly wouldn't expect you to have the things fixed in twelve hours, no matter how fanatical they are."

"I thought—"

"You didn't think." He had enough control by now to touch her again, so he gave her a gentle push toward the door. "Go inside, will you? If it's that important to you, I'll take care of hiding the lights."

"Not without someone holding the ladder." She shot the words back at him. "That's what you said."

Somehow he didn't appreciate having his own words used against him. "Right. Fine." He repositioned the ladder, making sure it was right next to the window. "You hold. I'll fix."

Now was not the time to point out that she probably wasn't strong enough to hold the ladder if it started to fall. It didn't matter, because he could do this in his sleep.

He scrambled up. The shutters shrieked as he pulled them out to hide the light fixtures. If not for the protective mesh screening the window, they could have done this a lot more safely from the inside.

"Good enough."

He climbed back down again and grasped the ladder, the aluminum cold against his fingers. Laura hurried to help him lower it against the wall. A splatter of rain hit the pavement as they did so.

"Let's get inside." He wasn't going to wait for her to invite him in. He still had a few words to say to Laura, but they may as well be said someplace a little drier.

At least she didn't try to get rid of him. She hurried inside, ducking her head against the raindrops, and let him drag the ladder in and lock the back door. She was through the front room and halfway up the steps by the time he'd done that.

He followed more slowly. Was Laura trying to evade the scolding she no doubt knew he planned? Or just anxious to check on her daughter?

When he reached the second-floor living room, she was scooping up the sleeping child from the sofa.

"I'll put her to bed and be back in a minute," she murmured, avoiding his eyes.

He nodded. The television screen danced with a popular children's video. He found the remote and clicked it off. He didn't want singing animals as a counterpoint to the conversation they were about to have.

Not conversation. Lecture. His imagination replayed the scene he'd found when he'd walked into that concrete alley behind the house. He couldn't shut the image off the way he had the video.

Laura, clinging to the top of the swaying ladder. Laura, ready to smash to the pavement below.

He'd seen plenty of his fellow firefighters in danger. It had never affected him the way this had.

"I'm sorry."

He hadn't heard her come out of Mandy's room, but she stood a few feet away. Her dark eyes were so huge and apprehensive that some of the anger drained out of him.

"If you think an apology is going to save you from a lecture, you're wrong."

She shook her head. "I guess I shouldn't have tried it without someone to hold the ladder." The thread of defensiveness that underlay the words told him she wasn't ready to admit how foolish it had been. "Thanks for showing up when you did."

If he'd come sooner, she wouldn't have had to try it. That thought did nothing to ease the turmoil inside him. He crossed the space between them in a couple of steps and grasped her shoulders.

"You scared me, Laura. I know I don't have the right

to tell you what to do, but I don't want to see you get injured for the sake of a stupid light."

Especially one he'd put up. If he'd foreseen the problem, he'd have hidden the fixtures to begin with.

"I didn't get hurt."

"You could have." His fingers tightened, feeling the warmth of her skin and the firmness of her muscles under the soft cotton of her shirt. "Don't you see that?"

Her jaw set stubbornly, and again he had to resist the impulse to shake her. Instead he turned her around, marched her to Mandy's bedroom door, and eased it open.

The nightlight cast a yellow glow over the sleeping child. The even murmur of Mandy's breathing was the only sound. He eased the door closed again before he spoke.

"Tell me," he demanded. "What would happen to Mandy if something happened to you?"

She whitened as if he'd struck her. "That's not fair." The words came out in a soft gasp.

"I don't care about being fair as long as I can make you think." He clenched his fingers to keep from touching her again. "You're all that little girl has. She can't lose you, Laura."

Anger mixed with the tears that sparkled in her eyes. "Do you think I don't know that? Do you think it doesn't keep me up at night, wondering, worrying? She doesn't have anyone else. I have to take care of her."

Her pain seemed to wrap around his heart, penetrating as nothing else could. "I know." His voice went soft. "That's why you shouldn't take risks."

She took a few steps back into the living room, shaking her head. The wiry strands of her dark hair curled around her face, and she brushed them back impatiently.

"Don't you see? That's why I have to take risks," she said. "The risk of fixing this place up, the risk of going broke, the risk that the preservation committee is going to tie me up in red tape. I'm all Mandy has, and I have to do the right thing for her."

"I know you're worried about getting the house finished—" he began, not quite sure what was driving her.

"It's not just that. Mandy's whole future is at stake. I have to be able to pay for her surgery." She rubbed the back of her neck. "Ten days. That's all I have."

How would she react if he offered to lend her the money? Shoot him out of the water, probably. Not that he had that much to lend, but at least it would be a start. Maybe enough for the deposit the hospital required.

"What about a loan?"

"I've tried. The loan officer was polite enough not to laugh." She rubbed her neck again, and he could guess at the tension that had taken up residence there. "If I have a signed contract with my buyer, then they'd be happy to advance me the money. Of course, if I had that, I wouldn't need them, would I?"

"Maybe I could help."

She shook her head, as he'd known she would. "I don't borrow from friends."

"I want to help."

A faint smile teased her lips as she shot a glance at

him. "Admit it. Your bank account probably looks almost as bad as mine does."

The trace of a smile reassured him. Laura was bouncing back. That resilience of hers was probably the only thing that kept her going in spite of all the obstacles in her path.

"I'm sure the bank doesn't consider me one of their prime accounts, but what I have is yours." That sounded a little too personal. "For Mandy's sake. Besides, I know you're good for it."

The smile faded. "I'm not good for anything unless the sale goes through. There's barely enough to—" She stopped, clamping her lips shut.

"Laura—"

Careful, he warned himself. Don't get too close or she'll shut you out.

"I'm sorry. I know you said the building was all your husband left you, but I assumed there was insurance or something."

"Nothing. Like a lot of people, Jason figured he had plenty of time to worry about that." A shiver went through her, strong enough for him to see, and she rubbed her arms. "As it turned out, he didn't. A rainy night, an out-of-control driver on the Schuylkill Expressway, and there was no time left at all."

"I'm sorry." He'd never asked what happened to her husband. How dumb was that for someone who wanted to be a friend?

Her shoulders moved in what might have been a shrug, and she wrapped her arms around herself. "It's okay."

"No, it's not." He took a step closer. He wanted to touch her, to comfort her, but her body language warned him off. "I'm ashamed that I didn't realize how bad it was. You had to deal with the loss of the man you loved as well as the financial problems and your daughter."

Her face seemed to freeze. "That might be true. Except that Jason had killed whatever was left of our love a long time before he died."

For a moment Laura stood staring at Ryan, unable to believe the words had come out of her mouth. Then she turned away, her heart thudding in her chest.

She didn't talk about that. Didn't tell anyone about Jason, whether out of loyalty or a sense of her own failure she wasn't sure. She just didn't.

"Sorry." She managed to get the word out through a tight throat.

She heard Ryan's step behind her and felt his hands come down on her shoulders—strong, supporting.

"Don't be sorry." His deep voice had gone even deeper, as if he struggled with emotion, too. "I'm glad you said it."

"I don't talk about my marriage."

"Maybe you should." His grip tightened a little. "It seems to me you're carrying an awful lot on these shoulders, Laura. Wouldn't it ease the burden a little to share it with a friend?"

That calm offer of friendship was the best thing he could have done, she realized. Too much sympathy would have pitched her control out the window.

"Maybe. I don't know." She turned slowly to face him. "You didn't know Jason. If you had, you might see the situation differently."

"I might," he said. He took her hand and tugged her to the couch. "Come on. Sitting makes it easier to share confidences."

"What makes you think I'm going to share anything?" But she sat down next to him, hearing the comforting squeak of the couch springs, feeling the soft cushions curve around her like supporting arms.

"Because we're friends. Because you need to."

He was right about that. She did need to. She'd held it all inside for so long that the emotions roiled at the slightest touch. "Yes. I guess I do."

He put his hand over hers where it lay on the couch between them. "So talk to me about it. You loved him once," he prompted.

"Yes." She tried to remember how it had felt, but so many difficult times had come between. "We met in college. Jason was a year ahead of me. Popular, charming, smart. Everyone liked Jason."

She might have been describing Ryan back in high school. The flash of insight threw her off track. Was that what had attracted her to Jason—that superficial resemblance to the guy she'd had a crush on in high school?

Fortunately Ryan couldn't guess what she was thinking. "So you graduated, got married, started a life," he prompted.

"We bought a townhouse in Philadelphia. Jason's father helped us with the down payment. He said he didn't want us to live in a dump while we were starting out."

Was that when it had started—that constant interference in their lives? That constant gibing at Jason that he couldn't handle things on his own?

"That was nice of him. Or was it?" Ryan seemed to catch the mixed feelings in her tone.

"I don't know. Maybe he intended to be kind, but—" She shook her head. "I still don't understand the relationship between Jason and his father. I never did. I just know that Jason was always trying to prove he could handle things on his own. That he could be a better businessman than his father had ever been."

Ryan's fingers moved comfortingly on hers. "Fathers and sons can drive each other crazy. Their relationship wasn't your fault."

"I should have handled the situation better. But if I questioned anything Jason was doing, he acted as if I were criticizing him, just as his father did. So eventually he stopped telling me what he did." She swallowed. This was the hard part, and there was no point in confiding if she didn't say it. "Then Mandy was born."

Her throat closed. Ryan didn't say anything. He just waited.

"Jason hadn't wanted a baby, but if we were going to have one, it should have been a son. And it should have been perfect."

His hand tightened convulsively on hers. "How could he possibly look at that little girl and not fall in love with her?"

That was what she'd always thought, and she was immeasurably comforted to hear Ryan say the words.

"I don't know. I still don't understand. He just—turned us off. As if our marriage, our family, had been a business deal that went bad." She sucked in a breath. "I tried. I couldn't reach him."

"Did you separate?"

"No." Her mouth twisted. "We'd made vows I didn't intend to break. But he was away more and more. Business, he said. I didn't know until later that his father had cut him off. Too much money down too many bad deals."

"Surely the man wouldn't cut off his innocent granddaughter. It wasn't her fault that her father was…" He paused, seeming to delete several word choices. "…a disappointment."

Something else she'd never understood. "Your father wouldn't behave that way. Nor mine. Maybe that was where Jason got his attitude."

Ryan shook his head slowly. "I guess there are people like that. That doesn't mean I can understand them. Or accept their attitude."

"I tried to mend the breach, but there was nothing I could do. Then I found out Jason had been trying to solve his financial problems at the casinos in Atlantic City." It hurt to say, but the words seemed to push themselves out. "He was on his way there the night he was killed."

Ryan shifted his weight toward her. "I'm sorry. Sorry he died, sorry he was a jerk, sorry he didn't realize what he had in that beautiful little girl. In you."

She felt the heat rush to her cheeks and tried to deny it. She shouldn't let Ryan see how much his words meant to her.

"Well, that's my sad story, anyway. After I realized how little was left when the creditors had been paid, I went to Jason's father. I thought he'd surely be willing to lend me the money to get back on my feet. I was wrong."

Again she had the feeling that Ryan was editing his words before speaking.

"Maybe it's a good thing I don't know the man. I'd be tempted to do something that would land me in jail."

"You might be tempted, but you wouldn't." She could say that with confidence. "That's not who you are."

His fingers smoothed hers. "You must know me better than I know myself, then."

Maybe she did. At least she knew what a good heart he had underneath the charm he wore so casually. That was what Jason had been missing.

"So now you know." She tried to smile. "And you were right. It does feel good to tell a friend. Thank you."

"Any time." His voice lightened. "Burdens gladly shared, no charge. You'd do the same for me."

Would she? She'd lived absorbed in her daughter and her own problems for so long that maybe she'd lost the power to empathize with others.

"I hope so." She glanced up at his face, to find it nearer than she'd expected. Her heart gave a little hiccup, and she had to concentrate to keep her voice even. "I hope I can be as good a friend as you."

She expected the kind of light-hearted response Ryan

used to keep things on that smiling, surface level. But instead his blue eyes darkened until they were almost navy.

"You already are." His voice was a low, baritone rumble.

"I don't think I—" Whatever she might have said got lost on the way to her lips. She could only watch as his face drew nearer.

He was going to kiss her. She should turn away, she should stop this before it started—

His lips claimed hers, and she stopped thinking altogether. His arms closed around her warmly, his hands stroking her back, molding her against him.

She grasped his shoulders, feeling the strength and protectiveness that poured from him. Ryan cared. He might not want to admit it, but he cared.

"Laura." He brushed feather-light kisses across her cheek. "I'd hate to tell you how long I've wanted to do that."

She nestled her cheek against his. Take it lightly, some rational part of her mind warned. Just because he's attracted, just because he cares, that doesn't mean he will ever want anything more.

"You're not the only one." She leaned back in the circle of his arms, trying for a lightness she didn't feel. She patted his cheek. "This was the subject of my daydreams in high school, after all."

He smiled, the cleft in his chin deepening. "I was a dummy in high school."

She thought that was relief in his eyes at her light response. He didn't want her to overreact, after all.

That wasn't part of his persona. Nothing serious, nothing permanent, that was Ryan.

"I'd be tempted not to agree with that, but it's too late for an argument." She rose, turning away from him before her smile could slip and her expression showed him what she really felt for him.

He got up quickly. "You're right. I just intended to drop by and make sure you were okay."

"Instead you got stuck hearing my life story."

"Hey." He caught her arm, turning her to face him. "I don't regret anything that happened tonight." His fingers brushed her cheek, nearly undoing her.

"Thank you, Ryan. For everything." *It means more than you'll ever know.*

"I'll call you tomorrow, okay?"

"Okay."

She followed him down the stairs, grateful that the dim light hid any strain in her expression. At the outside door he paused. He bent to plant a kiss where his touch had been.

"I mean it. I'll call."

"I know."

He would call. She watched him walk away and then closed and bolted the door. But that didn't mean anything would come of it.

Ryan was attracted to her, but they were at entirely different places in their lives. With the best intentions in the world, there was no way lighthearted Ryan was ready for the complications involved in loving someone like her.

She'd better keep that firmly in mind if she didn't want to be hurt.

Chapter Nine

Laura watched Mandy run across the lawn at Gabe and Nolie's farm a couple of days later, wondering if she could actually do this. Mandy seemed happy enough now, but how would she react when her mommy started to leave?

This had been Ryan's idea, of course. She'd mentioned that she wanted to go to a country sale to try and pick up some shelves for the third-floor room. Discovering that the sale was being held only a few miles from the farm, he'd proposed that Mandy stay with Nolie while he borrowed Gabe's truck and went with Laura to the sale.

She'd have refused, but he'd brought it up in front of Mandy, and she'd been so happy at the idea of seeing the puppies again that she hadn't been able to say no.

Ryan fell into step with her as they crossed the soft grass to where Nolie was hugging Mandy. The farmhouse seemed to spread out welcoming arms to them, and tulips nodded brightly along the edge of the porch.

"Relax," he said. "Nolie will take good care of her. She's great with children."

"I know she will. I'm just not used to leaving Mandy with anyone."

He clasped her hand, swinging it lightly. "Now's a good time to start, don't you think?"

A week or two ago she'd have been angry at his pre- sumption, but they'd moved past that stage. And she did trust Nolie. Nolie and Mandy were talking already, hands moving quickly, faces expressive. Nolie sat on the step, bringing her face to Mandy's level.

Nolie looked up and smiled when they approached. "We're going to visit the puppies. You two can go ahead and leave now, if you're ready."

You two, Nolie had said, as if they were a pair. They weren't.

Ryan gave Nolie an affectionate hug. "Thanks for the loan of the truck. And for keeping this little girl oc- cupied. I think hunting for bargains would get pretty boring for her after awhile."

"My pleasure." Nolie's smile said that it really was a pleasure. "Mandy, say bye-bye to Mommy. She's going shopping, but she'll be back soon."

Mandy flung her arms around Laura in a throttling hug and then ran back to Nolie, tugging on her hand. "Puppies," she announced.

"Have a good time." Nolie waved and let herself be pulled toward the barn. Mandy was so excited that she didn't even look back.

"I guess she's going to be fine." The discovery left her feeling oddly flat.

"Pleased? Or disappointed?"

Ryan was a little too perceptive, but she couldn't help smiling as she followed him to the truck.

"Some of both, I guess. I was prepared for Mandy to be a little apprehensive, at least."

He held the door for her, and she gave the pickup truck a considering look. "Are you sure this is going to get us there and back?"

"Positive." He brushed at a little mud caked on the red fender. "It may not look like much, but Gabe keeps it in top-notch order."

When she still hesitated, he laughed and gave her a quick hug. "Trust me."

She climbed into the high seat, trying not to react to the feel of his arm around her. He'd hugged her the same way he'd hugged Nolie—affectionately, nothing more.

That was how he'd behaved since the night they'd kissed. He'd certainly been attentive, checking in a couple of times a day by phone or in person. But his attitude had been casual, as if that kiss had been nothing more than a gesture between friends.

Well, that was how she wanted it. Just friends.

A sidelong glance showed her his strong hands on the wheel, the corded muscles in his forearms under the folded-back sleeves of his plaid shirt. Attraction, that's all it was, she told herself firmly. Nothing more.

"Are you dressing for the part?" She nodded to his faded jeans and well-worn shirt. "I've never seen you wearing plaid before."

He grinned. "Might as well try to fit in. We're looking for bargains, remember."

"The cheaper the better." The cash she'd tucked into her handbag would have to be enough, because it was all she could spare.

With a spray of gravel, Ryan turned the truck around and pulled out onto the country road. "We're off. Hope they have what you want."

"According to the sale list, they have several sets of wooden shelves. I just hope the sale isn't cluttered with dealers, jacking the prices up."

"That's not usually a big problem around here. This is far enough from the city that prices stay reasonable."

She nodded, checking her bag to be sure her cell phone was on in case Nolie needed to call her.

"She's not going to call," Ryan said, reading her emotions again. His hands moved easily on the wheel. "The only problem you're going to have is getting Mandy away from those puppies without taking one home. You should, you know. Every kid needs a pet."

She slid the cell phone back into place a little guiltily. "That's easy enough for you to say. You know where you'll be living in a month or two. We might end up in a rental that doesn't allow pets."

"Plenty of apartments do."

"And plenty of them don't." She tried to put finality in her tone.

"Look, I know you think I'm bugging you about this."

Ryan pulled into a narrow gravel lane marked by a white board that bore a single word: Sale. The word slanted slightly downhill, as if the artist wasn't used to painting letters, and the black paint trailed a wavy line under the *e*.

"You *are* bugging me," she pointed out.

He turned into a field and pulled into a parking space next to an SUV. "Only because I think it would give you and Mandy a little more protection."

His face was so serious that her heart jolted.

"Why do you think we need more protection? Have you found out something else about the arsonist?"

"Only that he's covering his trail well." He frowned. "Too well."

"If you're trying to scare me, you're succeeding." The thought that the unknown person might come back to finish his job was never far from her mind.

Ryan shrugged, broad shoulders moving under the plaid shirt. He looked uneasy. "I want you to be careful, not scared. Maybe I'm letting North's attitude influence me too much. He sees trouble around every corner."

"So do I, lately." How could she help it?

"Well, let's both try to put that situation on the back burner for today. We can't do anything about it now." He opened the door and slid out. "Let's go see if we can find some bargains."

She followed him across the stubbly grass of the field, analyzing what he'd said. If Ryan did know something else about the arsonist, would he tell her? Probably not. That was the line between friendship and business for him.

Well, today was about business for her, and she'd best concentrate on that. Her mind flickered to Mandy.

Is she all right without me? Lord—

She stopped abruptly, startled at herself. At one time in her life she'd carried on that sort of constant conversation with God. Then the grudge she bore put a stop to those almost unconscious prayers.

I'll pray for you.

People like the Flanagans said those words so easily. For all she knew, Mandy was in someone's prayers right now. But not her mother's.

The thought shook her, and she tried to push it away. It wouldn't go.

Ryan stopped, glancing at her. "Something wrong?"

"No." *I just don't know where I am, or whether God even wants to hear from me.*

She knew how Siobhan would answer that. *Of course He does. He's never stopped loving you.*

But Siobhan had more faith than she did.

The items for sale sat in haphazard rows in the mowed field next to the barn, looking like so many forlorn tombstones. Yellow stickers announced hoped-for prices, but she suspected no price was firm. People who had estate sales wanted to get rid of things.

She paused by a stack of old family photograph albums, their pages sliding apart. Sad, that there was no one left in the family who wanted them. Maybe the family line had died out. Or no one cared.

Ryan had passed the photo albums without a glance and was kneeling next to a cardboard box filled with eight-track tapes. "Hey, look at this great collection."

She shook her head, amusement replacing that faint sense of melancholy. "It's only great if you have something to play them on. Do you own an eight-track player?"

He rose, dusting his hands off. "Actually there just might be one in the attic. Dad keeps threatening to get a Dumpster and get rid of our junk, but he never does. He knows there's just as much of his old stuff up there as ours."

"It must be nice to have lived in the same house for so long."

"Three generations of Flanagans. Four, actually, counting Seth's little boy, but they'll be moving out soon, when Seth and Julie get married." His eyebrows lifted. "Didn't you stay put, when you were a kid? I remember the house you lived in on Maple."

"We moved from there when I was fifteen. My mother wanted something a little bigger."

"Bigger? There were only three of you."

"She really wanted something a little more prestigious." She grimaced. "She thought moving to a more upscale neighborhood would give me what she called 'the right kind of friends.'"

"Did it?"

She bent to examine an old sewing-machine cabinet, hoping to hide her face. "No."

She'd just been more alone. Her mother had never understood that Laura wasn't capable of the kind of social success she'd wanted. It had been one more cause for disappointment in her daughter.

"I guess she didn't approve of ordinary middle-class people like the Flanagans." He gave her that lopsided grin.

"I've never noticed anything ordinary about the Flanagans." She managed a smile, eager to move away from the subject of her mother.

"That's because there were so many of us." He glanced past her, attention diverted. "Look at that."

She took one look and fell in love. A child's dresser sat crookedly in the grass. The triple mirror was cracked and the white paint chipped, but it had beautifully turned legs and a curved top.

"It's darling." She touched the roses carved around the mirror. "But in terrible shape."

"There's a matching chair." Ryan picked up the child's chair, turning it in his capable hands. "A spindle is missing and the glue's dried out, but it's nothing that can't be fixed. Wouldn't Mandy love this?"

She glanced at the price. "Probably, but I can't afford to buy anything more than I have to get today. Anyway, I don't have the time to fix it up just now."

Ryan didn't seem to be paying attention. He lifted one hand, and a stout elderly woman approached, jingling the change in the white denim apron she wore. She'd probably been watching them, eagle-eyed, scenting a buyer.

"Help you folks with something?"

"Ryan, I don't want to buy that today." What part of no didn't the man understand?

"I'm interested in the little dresser." He did a great job of ignoring her. "If you think you can do a bit better on the price."

The woman gave a show of reluctance. "That was my mother's when she was a little girl. I bet I could get more than that for it from an antique shop."

"Maybe so, but I'm here now." Ryan gave her the smile that had been melting feminine hearts all his life. "And I know a little girl who'd love it as much as your mother did."

She wavered. "Well—"

"Tell you what." Ryan pulled some bills from his wallet. "You throw in the chair, and I'll meet your price on the dresser."

"Guess you got a deal." She snatched the money, and it disappeared into her apron pocket. She glanced from Ryan to Laura. "Hope your little girl likes it."

"She will," Ryan said confidently.

The woman trudged off toward a couple who lingered over a cast-iron bedstead, and he turned to her with a grin. "I got a deal."

"I told you I couldn't buy it today."

"You didn't. I did. And I'll fix it up for her." He caught her hand. "Come on, Laura. Admit that you're pleased about it."

He looked like a kid who'd succeeded in robbing the cookie jar. She couldn't help but succumb.

"All right. I'm pleased. You did a nice thing." She closed her fingers around his.

He put his other hand atop their clasped fingers, holding it warmly. That warmth traveled right up her arm and blossomed in her heart.

She looked up at him, knowing he'd be able to read the feelings in her face but unable to resist. The dense blue of his eyes darkened, and his breath rasped. If they hadn't been standing in the middle of a field they'd have been in each other's arms.

She took a step back. It wasn't just her. Ryan felt that dangerous attraction, too. And he was holding back, just as she was.

Laura ought to be happy with the results of the sale, Ryan figured. She'd found just the right shelves for the third-floor room, and at a great price, too.

Ryan glanced across at her as the truck bumped down the lane to the farm. At the moment she scribbled in a notebook, frowning a little. Maybe she was adding up all the things she still had to do. Or how much she'd spent.

And he'd bought a child's dresser and chair. He still couldn't explain to himself why he'd done it. He'd just felt drawn to the piece, as if it had been sitting in the grass waiting for him.

He wanted to do something that would bring that shy smile to Mandy's face. Mandy needed to know that someone besides her mother would go out of the way to make her happy.

Laura had revealed more than she'd intended to, probably, the night she'd told him about her husband's reactions to Mandy's birth. He'd wanted a boy. He'd wanted a perfect child.

Ryan discovered he was gripping the wheel so tightly that his knuckles were white. If the man weren't dead, he'd like to give him an attitude adjustment.

Sorry. I got carried away. But surely God understood a bit of righteous anger on behalf of one of His little ones.

How could Mandy's father have looked at that precious child and not loved her? Even a stranger like him—

Well, maybe it was better not to explore too fully his feelings for Laura and her child.

Still, he could certainly understand Laura's protectiveness toward Mandy. Over-protectiveness, he'd thought at times. He'd wanted to say something, but he hadn't. And he wouldn't.

For one thing, he didn't have that right, not unless he was ready to make a far more serious commitment than he ever had in his life.

And for another, Laura just plain wouldn't tolerate anyone's interference where her daughter was concerned. He'd rather take on a five-alarm blaze than face that maternal instinct.

"Here we are," he announced unnecessarily, pulling up under the willow tree. "Looks like a welcoming committee is waiting for us."

Nolie stood by the door, holding Mandy's hand. When he turned the engine off, she let go. Mandy raced across the lawn and into Laura's arms. Laura's cheek pressed against her daughter's, and their dark hair mingled.

Ridiculous to have a lump in his throat. Especially when Nolie was watching him with a knowing look that reminded him too much of his mother.

"Hey, how about a hug for me, too?" He knew enough signs to get that across.

Mandy grinned and launched herself at him. His throat tightened again at the feel of those little arms around his neck. Her father had been an idiot. He could have had this, and he hadn't wanted it.

Nolie approached at a more reasonable pace, one of the dogs dancing around her.

"How was Mandy while we were gone? Did she seem upset at all?" Laura seemed to realize how that sounded, and she shook her head with a rueful smile. "Sorry. I know you took good care of her."

"She was fine. We played with the puppies and had lunch. After lunch Mandy helped feed the horses. Then we read some stories." Nolie gave Mandy a quick hug. "Mandy's really a good helper. She can come to visit any time."

Mandy grinned, pride brightening her face.

"How was the sale?" Nolie asked. "Did you find what you wanted?"

Laura gestured toward the bed of the truck. "As you can see. The shelves will be perfect once they're painted."

"I see you got something that wasn't on the list." Nolie peered into the truck bed, smiling. "That's the trouble with sales. Every time I go to one, I end up buying something I just have to have."

"I didn't buy it," Laura said quickly. "Ryan was the one who couldn't resist."

"Right. I'm the sucker." He hoisted Mandy up so that she could see into the truck. "See, Mandy? I bought that for your room. A dresser and chair just like grown-up ladies have."

Mandy pointed to her chest, eyebrows lifting.

"That's right, sweetheart." Laura touched her daughter's cheek to get her attention. "Ryan bought it for you, and he's going to fix it up so it'll be really pretty."

Mandy just looked at him for a moment. Then she threw her arms around his neck again. This time he knew it wasn't his neck she was squeezing. It was his heart.

He set her down carefully, ruffling her hair and trying not to look at that thought. He couldn't actually love Laura's child. If he did—well, that way lay responsibility for another human being's life. He wasn't ready for that. He wasn't capable of that.

"Maybe we ought to get this stuff back to your house. I'd like to return the truck before dark."

Laura nodded, but Mandy shook her head so that her hearing aid cords bounced against her neck.

"Puppies," she announced, tugging at Laura's hand.

Nolie laughed. "I don't think you're going to get away without Laura looking at the puppies again. It'll only take a minute."

"Right." Laura clasped her daughter's hand. "Let's go see the puppies one more time."

He started to go after them, but before he could take a step, Nolie grabbed his arm.

"Hang on a sec, Ryan. I want to talk to you about something."

He nodded. Mandy glanced back over her shoulder at him, and he waved to her before turning to his sister-in-law. "What's up?"

The words came out lightly, but then he saw her expression and his heart clenched. "What is it? What's wrong? Is it Gabe?" His brother hadn't had a seizure in months, but they all knew it could happen any time.

"No, nothing like that." Nolie took a breath. "It's Mandy."

"Mandy," he repeated, mind churning. "Did something go wrong today you don't want to tell Laura about?"

"Not exactly."

He lifted his eyebrows at her reluctance. "Come on, Nolie. You're well-known for your plain speaking. Spit it out, whatever it is."

"It's none of my business." She gave a rueful smile. "But I guess that's not going to stop me. Mandy seemed to feel comfortable with me. Comfortable enough to talk to me about the implant."

He still didn't understand what had put that concern in her eyes. "That's good, isn't it? She probably wanted a little reassurance."

"It wasn't exactly good. What Mandy said is that she's afraid of the implant. She doesn't want it."

He sucked in a breath. "Are you sure? I mean—"

"My signing skills are equal to understanding that." Nolie's blue eyes were troubled. "I did try to reassure her, but I don't think it did much good. I'm not the one she needs to be hearing it from."

"No." His heart sank. "Laura's trying so hard to do the best thing for her. I guess she thinks Mandy is as positive about the procedure as she is."

"Kids sometimes hide their feelings from the people they're closest to. But Laura has to be told."

"Right."

"And you have to be the one to tell her."

"Contrary to my reputation for irresponsibility, I actually figured that one out."

Nolie patted his cheek. "You're not irresponsible, Ryan. Just a little evasive."

Evasive when it came to commitment, she meant. Nolie, as usual, had hit the nail on the head.

This was one emotional encounter he couldn't evade. Laura had to be told about Mandy's fears, and he had to be the one to tell her.

And given her feelings about people interfering in her life, it wasn't going to be a pleasant experience.

Chapter Ten

"Watch your step." The warning came out of Laura's mouth involuntarily as they heaved the last of the shelf units up the steps to the third floor.

"I never would have thought of that if you hadn't told me." Ryan didn't sound as breathless as she did, even though his muscles bunched as he maneuvered the awkward piece through the narrow doorway at the top of the stairs.

Her breath came out with a whoosh of relief as they slid the heavy shelves against the nearest wall. She stood back to admire her purchase.

"That's the last one. It's a good thing because I couldn't have managed any more." She ran her hand along the dusty cherry shelf. "They're going to be perfect, aren't they?"

"Definitely. I told you this was going to be your lucky day at the sale."

"Thanks, Ryan. I couldn't have done this without your help."

Her own words startled her. She didn't normally say that, even think it.

But it was true. No matter how much she wanted to do everything on her own, sometimes she needed help. Maybe her friendship with Ryan and his family had made it easier to accept that.

"Hey, no problem. I enjoyed it, except for the heavy loading part." Ryan wiped his forehead with his sleeve and stood looking around the room. "I wouldn't have believed it, but this space is really shaping up. The shelves will finish it off perfectly."

She nodded. "Except for that wall." She knocked her fist in frustration at the partition which still stood, mocking her. "The contractor promised me he'd be here days ago. I'll have to call him again."

"Promises are easy. Living up to them is the tough part. Your dad may have been the last contractor in Suffolk who actually showed up when he promised."

"He's always been a man of his word." She had to smile, remembering how often her father had been called in to fix another contractor's botched job or finish something someone else had left undone. "If I'd had my choice, I'd have taken over the business when he retired."

"Why didn't you? You'd have been great."

"My mother wouldn't hear of that." She grimaced. "It wasn't the life she imagined for her daughter."

Ryan leaned against the wall, his long body relaxing. He always seemed able to relax at a moment's notice. Maybe that was a firefighter characteristic.

"Didn't you and your father outnumber her?" He

sounded genuinely interested in how her family had worked. Or not worked, in this case.

"Somehow it never turned out that way." She remembered only too well the tears, the palpitations, the sick headaches that resulted whenever something had threatened the plans her mother made. "I guess we were in the habit of giving in to her."

"It's not good for people always to get their way." He grinned. "And that's coming from someone who's tried it, believe me."

His insight startled her. Would her mother have been a better person if she and her father had stood up to her on occasion? She'd never thought of it that way. Maybe so, but it was too late to change anything now.

"Well, it's getting late." She glanced at her watch. "I'd better let you go. I know you want to take the truck back to the farm before dark."

Ryan pushed away from the wall in an easy, fluid movement. "It's not that late. How about if I go pick up a pizza for our supper?"

Was there a polite way of saying she was bushed and would rather have a bowl of cereal and collapse on the couch? Probably not.

He seemed to sense her hesitation. "Come on. You owe me supper after all that heavy labor. What do you and Mandy like on your pizza?"

He started down the steps, apparently taking her acceptance for granted.

"Plain for us, please."

She descended a little more slowly, hearing the thumping of his steps. The front door slammed behind him.

Funny. Given that Ryan seemed to be trying as hard as she was not to give in to the attraction between them, she'd expected him to make an excuse to leave as soon as possible. That probably would have been the smartest thing, for both of them.

Well, they'd cope. Maybe it would get easier to pretend that she didn't want anything but friendship.

Her mind switched back to Mandy. Could she get Mandy bathed and into her pajamas before Ryan returned with the pizza? Her little girl had had a full day, too.

As it happened, she actually had time to clean herself up, too; she was toweling her damp hair when Ryan reappeared, balancing two flat white pizza boxes.

"Two?" Her eyebrows lifted. "Looks like an awful lot of pizza for three people."

"Hey, I'm hungry after all that manual labor. I'll eat my share." He slid the boxes onto the cherry drop-leaf table in the corner of her living room next to the tiny galley kitchen. "Dig in, ladies."

Mandy, looking ready for bed in her princess pajamas, waited until she saw which chair Ryan was going to take and then slipped onto the one next to him. Ryan handed her a slice of pizza.

She watched gravely as he took his. She mimicked his motions as he scooped up a slice, curving it so that no cheese escaped.

It looked as if her little daughter had fallen for Ryan, as females of all ages did. Laura frowned as she took a bite of her slice. That sort of attachment was something she'd hoped to avoid. She didn't want Mandy to learn to love someone who might walk out of their lives at any moment.

"Something wrong with the pizza?" Ryan's eyes were questioning.

"It's fine." She took another bite, enjoying the burst of cheese and tomato on her tongue. "Just thinking."

He nodded, accepting that, and turned to tease Mandy about the smear of tomato on her chin. Something in her eased at the gentle way he had of making Mandy smile. Ryan was one of the good guys. He'd never intentionally hurt them.

But Ryan's easy banter seemed a little strained as they ate, as if some concern hid itself behind his laughter. Something about the arson investigation? If so, she couldn't assume he'd tell her.

She glanced at Mandy to find her daughter drooping over her plate. She reached over to remove it before cheese adorned the pajamas.

"You go brush your teeth and get into bed, sweetheart. I'll be there in a minute to tuck you in."

Mandy nodded, sliding off her chair. She hesitated, looking up at Ryan, and then went up on tiptoe to kiss his cheek. Before he could react, she scampered off toward the bathroom.

"You've made a conquest," she said lightly. She began folding up the boxes.

Ryan took them from her. "I think it's the other way around. Do you mind if we talk for a minute?"

"Of course not." A frisson of apprehension flicked her nerves at the gravity of his tone. "What is it?"

He frowned down at the boxes as if he'd never seen

them before stuffing them into the kitchen trash can. He walked back to her, planting both hands on the table as if to brace himself for something unpleasant.

"Something happened today while Mandy was at Nolie's," he said flatly.

"But Nolie said she was fine." Laura's mind skittered after possibilities and came up empty. "What went wrong?"

"Nothing went wrong," he said quickly. "But Mandy told Nolie something that we feel you ought to know."

His reluctance was so palpable that she knew it was something he thought would hurt her.

"Whatever it is, just tell me." Her voice was tart. "Don't dance around it."

"Right." He took a breath. "Okay, here it is. Mandy told Nolie that she's afraid of the implant. She doesn't want to get it."

She could only stare at him. "But—that's crazy. Nolie must have misunderstood her."

"Nolie wouldn't make a mistake like that. That's what Mandy told her."

She shook her head, unable to take it in. "But I've explained about the implant to Mandy. She knows she'll be able to hear after she has the procedure. Why would she say something like that?"

"Maybe she doesn't really understand what it means to be able to hear. Or maybe it's the procedure that scares her. She's only five."

Her anger flared, penetrating the shock. "I know how old my daughter is. Do you think you understand her better than I do?"

"Of course not. Nolie doesn't either. We just thought—"

"You thought you should interfere."

Ryan seemed to absorb her anger, rather than bouncing it back against her.

"We thought you should know, Laura." He looked at her gravely, all his usual easy charm submerged in his concern. "That's all. We're just trying to help."

The kindness in his eyes deflated her. The brief anger fizzled away, to be replaced by despair.

Failure.

She took a choked breath. "She really feels that way?" It came out as a whisper.

"She doesn't understand." His voice was very gentle. "She needs reassurance. From you."

From her mother, the one person who should have known what she was feeling. *Am I that heedless a mother?* It took a moment to realize who she was asking. *Am I?*

A tremor went through her. If she failed Mandy, nothing else that she did would be worth anything.

Help me. Please.

Ryan stood in the living room, unsure whether to stay or go. Laura had looked at him with that desperate, stricken expression, and then she'd spun around and hurried into Mandy's room.

He'd hurt her. But how could he have handled the situation any differently? She'd needed to know the truth about Mandy's feelings in order to deal with them.

Maybe she'd eventually be grateful to him, but he

couldn't quite convince himself of that. Most people weren't grateful to those who brought them bad news, no matter how much they needed to hear it.

He wanted to leave. Actually moved toward the stairs, but something held him back.

Leave. Go. Run. That was how he dealt with anything emotional. He'd become an expert at evasion.

Mandy and Laura were different. He couldn't go without knowing they were all right.

Laura had left the door to Mandy's room open. Maybe on purpose, maybe because she'd been too distraught to think of closing it. Mandy was visible past the edge of the door. He could see Laura, hear her soft voice as she tucked the quilt around her daughter.

She sank down on the bed next to Mandy, her body curving as she leaned protectively over her child. Every line of her figure radiated maternal love, a force so strong that it would sweep anything from its path.

"Ryan says you're worried about the implant, sweetheart." Her hands moved slowly, as if they were reluctant to form the words. "Is that right?"

Mandy looked down at her hands, picking at the star design on the quilt. Then she nodded.

"Mandy, it's okay to tell Mommy that." Laura stroked Mandy's dark curls. "I want to know when you're worried or upset about something."

Mandy looked up, and her fingers moved. I'm scared. He knew that sign.

Laura drew her closer. "It's okay to be scared. Honest. Sometimes Mommy is scared of things, too."

And Ryan?

The innocent words hit him right in the heart. Did he really matter that much to Mandy?

"Let's ask him," Laura said, her voice a little husky. "Ryan, will you come in?"

No running away now. He marched into the room, wondering why this should be more frightening than advancing into a fully involved structure.

He stood next to the twin bed, smiling down at the small figure. "I get scared, too, Mandy."

Her hands moved in something he didn't catch. He looked at Laura.

"She says you're a firefighter. Firefighters don't get scared."

"Yes, we do. Honest. Especially when we have to do something we've never done before."

"Is that what scares you?" Laura asked. "Going into the hospital when you haven't ever done that before?"

Mandy nodded. *I don't want to.*

"I'm sorry. I didn't know you were scared about it." It probably took a lot of effort for Laura to keep her voice that even. "But it's going to be okay, honest. When you go to the hospital, Mommy will go, too."

And Ryan?

The least he could do was keep a smile on his face, even if his heart seemed to be doing something strange.

"I'll come to the hospital to see you. I promise. I'll even bring you a special firefighter teddy bear to keep you company."

Mandy looked solemnly from him to Laura. She touched her ears and signed something he didn't quite catch.

Laura's eyes shone with tears. "I'll love you if you hear or if you don't hear. I loved you before you were born, and I'll never stop loving you."

Maybe that was what Mandy needed. She threw her arms around Laura's neck. Laura folded her into a tight embrace, the tears spilling onto her cheeks.

He should leave them alone. But before he could take a step back, Mandy held her arms out to him.

He bent to receive her hug, feeling his throat tight with unshed tears. It was way too late to back out now.

Laura managed to wipe the remnants of tears away before she rejoined Ryan in the living room. He hadn't left, and the relief she felt at that fact startled her. Did she really want to unload on him again? The poor man had probably had enough emotion for one night.

She pinned a smile on her face. The very least she owed him was her thanks. He'd done a difficult thing, telling her, knowing it would hurt her. So she'd thank him, and she'd let him go.

Ryan stood at the bookshelf, looking at the photos of Mandy that adorned its top. He turned at her step, a lock of dark hair falling onto his forehead at the movement. He brushed it back impatiently.

"Is she all right?"

"I think so. Thanks to you." She tried to keep her smile steady. "I'm grateful, Ryan. To you and to Nolie. I know I didn't make it easy for you to tell me."

"It wasn't easy to hear, I guess." His gaze probed her face, as if he wondered how real her smile was.

"It certainly was the last result I expected from having Mandy stay at Nolie's today."

She moved closer, so she could see which photo he held. It was a recent one, taken the day Mandy had ridden the donkey at the farm. She and Ryan's niece laughed at the camera, clutching the donkey's neck.

"You shouldn't think—" He stopped, as if not sure he should go on. "Well, sometimes it's easier for kids to confide in someone they don't know too well."

"Instead of a parent." She finished the thought for him. "I'd have said there was nothing Mandy wouldn't tell me. I guess I was wrong."

He put the photo down. "Laura, you're a good mother. Don't criticize yourself for something you couldn't have foreseen."

"I should have seen it. I should have been paying more attention." She felt the prickle of tears in her eyes and tried to blink them away. She would not break down in front of him. "I was so obsessed with my own plans for Mandy that I didn't take the time to find out how she was feeling."

"You were doing your best." He turned, taking her shoulders in a firm, comforting grasp. "Nobody can do more than that."

"I should have."

His hands tightened. "You're only one person, and you've been trying to do the work of six or seven."

He was giving her an out, but she couldn't take it.

"Mandy has to come first. She doesn't have anyone but me. I have to be responsible."

"You are." He pulled her gently against him, as if a

hug might convince her when words didn't. "Stop beating yourself up over it, Laura. You're a good mother. Once you knew what the problem was, you took care of it. Everything's going to be all right."

She'd like to believe that. Oh, how she'd like to believe it. With Ryan's strong arms around her, she almost could.

She leaned against his chest, feeling the steady beating of his heart against her cheek. This was what was missing in her life—this sense that someone was in on the task with her, standing by her side, being strong when she was weak.

Ryan pressed a kiss against her temple. "Better?"

"Better." She stepped back, out of the comfort of his arms. "I'm fine. Thank you, Ryan."

"Any time." But his easy smile was strained, an imitation of the real thing. "You have the right to make a mistake once in a while, Laura. Or to need someone to lean on for a moment."

For a moment.

The phrase he'd used echoed in her mind. Was he trying to tell her something? That the moment was over?

She straightened her shoulders. "Single moms have to be independent. We don't have a choice."

It was a fine thing, being independent. Unfortunately it could also be a lonely thing.

"You're a responsible kind of person. Everyone knows I'm not, but I certainly recognize the quality when I see it."

Something sounded under the light words. It took a

moment to register that he'd voiced a similar idea before, the day he'd talked about his father's heart attack.

"What makes you say you're not a responsible person? You certainly seem pretty responsible to me."

He shrugged, turning away as if the subject made him uncomfortable. "I've always been reckless. Born that way, maybe. Or maybe I just picked it up, trying to keep up with my big brothers."

"You're not a little kid any longer. You don't have to prove anything to them."

"Maybe not, but old habits die hard." His smile flickered. "Anyway, Mandy's lucky she has someone like you, instead of someone like me."

It took a moment, but she got it. Ryan was warning her off. They'd gotten too close, and he wanted her to realize he wasn't the kind of guy for happily ever after.

Even as she returned his smile, she realized the warning had come too late. Much too late.

She'd fallen in love with Ryan, and there wasn't a thing she could do about it.

Chapter Eleven

He shouldn't be going to see Laura again. Ryan had left headquarters intending to get lunch, hopped in the car, and found himself driving down her street.

After the way he'd left things with her the night before, he ought to head in the opposite direction. He could stop by the station house to see whether there was a pot of chili on the stove. It would certainly cause him less heartburn than reflecting on his mistakes with Laura.

Laura had opened up to him. She'd let him into her life, into her daughter's life, in a way he'd never expected. And he'd responded by warning her off.

Seth had been right all along. He shouldn't get involved with Laura and Mandy unless he was in it for the long haul. The very thought terrified him. How did anyone do that—commit to another person emotionally for life? It was like jumping off the roof of a burning building.

No, it was worse. He wouldn't be afraid of jumping off a roof. He was terrified by the thought of taking responsibility for the happiness of two other people.

He shouldn't be driving down her street, pulling to a stop at the curb, but he had to be sure they were all right. After the pain he'd caused Laura the night before, he had to check on them.

And when he'd done that, he'd start backing his way slowly but surely out of their lives.

Mandy sat in a patch of sunshine on the sidewalk, drawing a picture with chalk, while Laura sat on the step, painting the wrought-iron railing of the stoop a shining black. They both looked up and smiled at his approach, and his heart clutched. Walking away wasn't going to be easy.

"Hi, Mandy." He squatted next to her, ruffling her dark curls. "That's a really pretty picture."

She'd drawn a house—a square with a peaked roof, a chimney, and smoke coming out. He remembered doing the same picture at that age. But where his had had the lengthy line-up of stick figures representing his parents and his siblings, hers had only a yellow puppy.

She nodded, carefully adding a bird to the sky.

He stood, dusting off his uniform pants, and met Laura's eyes. "How is it going?" He nodded toward Mandy. "Any more worries last night?"

"Not at all. She slept fine and woke up happier than I've seen her in a while."

"That's good." He couldn't help taking the few steps to her. "I'm glad."

"I owe it to you." She tilted her head back, shading

her eyes from the sunlight with a paint-daubed hand. "I can't believe I didn't realize something was bothering her."

"You're not going to start blaming yourself again, are you?"

She smiled ruefully. "I won't. I promise. But thank you, Ryan."

The words were simple, but the way she was looking at him wasn't. It would take a better man than he was to walk away from a look like that.

Okay, time to regroup. Talk about something—anything—that wasn't emotional.

"The railing looks great. You're really down to the finishing touches on the house, aren't you?"

She nodded, probably realizing what he was trying to do. "Everything's shaping up the way I want it. The only frustrating thing is that the contractor still hasn't come to take out that wall on the third floor. I must have called him twenty times. You'd think he'd come just so he'd stop hearing from me."

"Sure you don't want me to bring a couple of guys over from the station house to knock it down for you? Firefighters are pretty good at tearing down walls."

Her lips twitched. "Thanks, but I find the thought of fire axes going after my wall a little scary."

"Suit yourself, but we do nice work. All our clients say so."

She probably didn't want to feel obligated to anyone else, and he'd try to respect that. Still, it wouldn't hurt to drop in on the contractor. He knew the guy slightly—maybe he could light a fire under him.

That wasn't really taking on responsibility. And anyway, Laura need never know he'd interfered.

She frowned at the railing and touched up a spot with the glossy black. "At least the front of the house is looking good. I'm going to stop by the farmers' market later and pick up some red geraniums to put in the window boxes."

She'd obviously given a fresh coat of paint to the boxes on the tall narrow windows that flanked the front door. They gleamed with the same shining black as the railing.

"I have to hand it to you, Laura. I'd never have believed, a month ago, that this place could look so good."

"It had better be looking good. I've heard from the woman who has an option to buy. She's coming on Friday to look at it."

She was smiling, so she obviously considered that good news.

"That's great." He tried to respond in kind. "You think you're going to be ready?"

She nodded. "With a little help from the contractor, I will be. I've told her about the damage to the back porch, so she won't be shocked by that. I'm hoping she'll visualize her business here so clearly that she'll overlook any little flaws and we can go to contract."

That meant she and Mandy would move out. With the house completed, she wouldn't need any more help. And he wouldn't have any reason to stop by.

That was as it should be. The fact that it left him feeling flat had no bearing on what he should do.

"She'll love it." His voice sounded falsely hearty, but

maybe she didn't notice. At a movement from the house next door, he glanced over Laura's head. "Well, well. Look who's coming."

Actually, Brad Potter might not be coming to see Laura. There was a slight hesitation in his step when he saw them.

Then the moment was gone, and he came toward them smoothly. Everything about the man was smooth, from the expensive cut of his shirt to the smile he aimed at Laura.

"Laura, how nice to see you." He reached out, as if to shake hands, and then took a quick step back from the wet paint.

Didn't want to get his hands dirty. Well, that was okay, as long as he hadn't come to cause Laura any more grief.

"How you doing, Brad? You don't have any more lists hidden in your pocket, do you?" That came out a little more sarcastically than he'd intended.

Laura sent him a sharp warning look.

"No, nothing like that." Brad's smile was hearty. He was Mr. Congeniality today, it seemed. "Laura has certainly been one of the more cooperative homeowners we've ever had the pleasure of working with on a project."

"If all goes well, I won't be the homeowner much longer. You'll have someone else to deal with." Laura sounded as if she couldn't keep her good news to herself.

Well, who was he to feel annoyed that she wanted to share the turn of events with Brad? She probably thought he'd be interested.

Which he seemed to be. He leaned toward Laura, heedless of the fresh paint. "You have a buyer already?"

"I have someone who has an option to buy." Caution sounded in her reply. "She'll be arriving on Friday, so I'm hoping to have a deal in place soon."

"Is this someone who plans to live in the house?" Brad's question came out sharply. It was impossible to tell what he was thinking, with his eyes shielded by those designer sunglasses.

Laura nodded. "She intends to have a vintage clothing shop on the first floor. It should make a lovely addition to the shops in the block."

"Well, that is good news." Brad took a step back, apparently mindful again of that wet paint. "I'm happy to hear it's working out so well for you after all the obstacles you've had to overcome."

"Thank you." Laura was graciousness itself, given the fact that Potter and his committee had provided many of the obstacles.

He supposed he shouldn't mention that. Maybe his face showed some of what he was thinking, though, because Potter gave him an uneasy glance and then lifted his hand.

"Congratulations on a job well done. I hope I'll see you again soon." He turned and strode off down the street.

Laura sat back on her heels and put her paint brush on the lid of the can. She looked up at Ryan with a challenge in her dark eyes.

"Did you have to be so rude to him? I thought you and Bradley Potter were old pals."

"Are you kidding? He wouldn't hang around with the likes of the Flanagans."

He caught himself up. If Brad was disposed to be friendly toward Laura, he shouldn't interfere. Especially when he'd decided it was time he backed out of her life.

"Brad's okay," he conceded. "Pretty successful, really. Rumor has it his old man ran through the family money, but Brad's put together a nice real estate business since he took over."

She nodded, but he could tell she was only giving Brad Potter a fraction of her attention. "At least he's not hassling me about the renovation anymore."

He glanced at his watch. His lunch hour was about up, and his stomach reminded him that he hadn't eaten anything.

"Well, maybe I'd better hit the road. Good luck with the buyer." In other words, he didn't expect to see her before then.

"Wait a second." She stood, wiping her hands on her jeans. "There's something I'd like to ask you."

"Sure. What?"

"I'm inviting a few people over for dinner tonight. Just a very casual meal, as a thank-you to people who've helped me. I know this is last-minute, but I hope you'll come."

He should invent some previous engagement. Back away, remember?

Before he could find an appropriate answer, a shrill noise startled him. Then he realized she'd put her cordless phone on the front step.

"Just a second, okay?" She picked up.

Not wanting to stand next to her while she talked, he moved over to look at Mandy's chalk drawing. She smiled up at him, clearly inviting him to admire her work.

She'd added to the picture. A little girl with dark curls now stood next to the dog, holding hands with a woman whose hair was equally dark. Mandy and her mother, obviously.

But that wasn't all. On the child's other side, she held hands with what was meant to be a male figure.

He'd tell himself that she was remembering her father, but he couldn't. Because the male figure wore what was obviously intended to be a navy-blue uniform.

For a moment he couldn't react at all. He glanced at Laura. Engrossed in the call, she hadn't noticed what Mandy had been drawing.

He couldn't tell a child that the image grabbed his heart. Or that it made him want to run away.

"Great picture, Mandy." He bent down and hugged her. "You're really good at drawing."

That probably wasn't what she wanted him to say, but it was the best he could manage.

Laura had hung up the phone, but she stood looking at it with an expression that startled him.

"Laura, what is it? Is something wrong?"

"No. Not wrong." She glanced at Mandy, and he realized she was being careful of what she said in front of the child. "That was the appointments desk at the hospital. They've had a cancellation. We're now on the schedule for Thursday."

He looked at Mandy, too, but she had turned back to her drawing, clearly not understanding the importance of that call.

"That's great, isn't it? Will you be able to manage the down payment by then?"

She looked so stunned that he stepped closer, taking her hand. It felt cold in his.

"Yes." She focused on him, joy dawning slowly in her eyes, as if she couldn't quite believe it was real. "It's wonderful. Soon, but wonderful. And Dr. Phillips convinced the hospital to let him go ahead, even though I won't have the down payment until at least next week."

"I'm glad." He squeezed her hand. "Looks like you've been getting some really overdue good news."

Her eyes shone with tears. "Silly, isn't it, to cry over something this good?"

"Not silly at all." He took a breath, realizing he wouldn't have to make up an excuse about her dinner after all. "Look, you won't want to be bothered with company tonight. I'm sure everyone will understand if you cancel."

She wiped the tears away impatiently. "Cancel? I'm not going to cancel. Now I really have something to celebrate, and it's nice to know I have friends to share it with. You're coming, aren't you?"

What could he say? "Sure, sounds great. I wouldn't miss it."

Everything seemed to be going well. Laura paused in the doorway of the kitchen, scanning the living room, crowded now with the people she'd invited. Flanagans, mostly, but a few others from the church. And Ryan's friend, Jerry White, the plasterer. All people to whom she owed a debt of gratitude.

The Flanagans, predictably, had insisted on bringing food with them. They'd set up card tables to augment her small dining table, spreading the food out buffet-style. People talked, ate, milled around the building admiring the changes accomplished in such a short time. The buzz of conversation, punctuated by laughter, filled the rooms.

It was odd, to be having her first and last party in the townhouse. Still, this night would be something to remember—a celebration of accomplishment and friendship.

Finding friendship had been the last thing on her mind when she'd come back to Suffolk. She'd thought she didn't have time, maybe didn't even have the capacity for friendship. She'd been proved wrong.

Thanks to Ryan. She didn't have to search for him in the crowded room. It seemed she'd developed a sort of radar where he was concerned. He stood over by the door, a plate in one hand, gesturing with it as he talked to his father. Or argued with him, maybe.

Those two might not look much alike, but they were, down deep where it counted, whether they realized it or not. Both strong, outgoing, passionate about what they did, physically unafraid.

She blinked, turning away, realizing she'd been staring too long. Her heart might ache with love for him, but Ryan must never know that. It would be a poor return for all the kindness he'd shown to make him feel uncomfortable about a love he couldn't return.

"Nice party." Pastor Brendan stopped next to her, balancing a dessert plate filled with two kinds of pie she certainly hadn't baked. Siobhan's handiwork, probably. "Lots of good food, good friends and good conversation."

She managed a smile, hoping he hadn't seen her watching Ryan. "I can't take credit for any of those. Everyone's managing the conversation on their own, and your family must have brought at least three-quarters of the food."

"They do enjoy bringing food." His intent gaze seemed to ask if that had offended her. "My Aunt Siobhan always figures you express love to someone by feeding them. She'd be hurt if you didn't let her help."

"Yes. Ryan told me once that his mother says God's hands on earth are other people."

Brendan's brows lifted. "You don't agree?"

"I guess I hadn't thought much about it." And thinking about it made her uncomfortable. "But certainly Siobhan lives by that, and she's taught her family to do the same."

"We haven't offered you charity, you know." Brendan seemed to read between the lines. That probably was an asset to a minister. "Just friendship."

"I know." That was all Ryan had to offer, and it would have to be enough. Too bad she wanted more.

"Ryan told me about Mandy's implant surgery." He reached out to take her hand in a firm, warm grip. "I'll be praying for her. And for you."

Her eyes filled with unexpected tears. "Thank you. I appreciate that." Those moments when she'd cried out in incoherent prayer flickered through her mind, and she pushed them away.

"Will it be all right if I stop in and see you and Mandy at the hospital Thursday?"

It would be difficult to say an outright no. "I don't want to take you out of your way."

"I'm there every day," he said gently. He squeezed her hand. "I'll see you then."

He moved away, apparently having said what he'd intended to say. She turned, thinking she'd replenish the serving trays, to discover that Ryan and his father had moved their argument, if that's what it was, to the buffet.

"Laura, tell me what you think about this stubborn son of mine." Joe seized her arm, making escape possible. "You've known him a long time. Maybe you can explain."

Ryan rolled his eyes, looking as embarrassed as she'd ever seen him. "Dad, give Laura a break. She doesn't want to take sides. You're just making her uncomfortable."

"Nonsense." Joe's booming voice turned several heads their way. "I just want to know what Laura thinks about you giving up a job you already do great to jump into something completely different."

"It's not completely different." Ryan sounded as if he'd said the words a few dozen times. "I'm still working for the fire department. I can even work shifts and go on calls when I'm not working a case."

"Working a case," Joe scoffed. "That makes you sound like a cop. All the time you were growing up, being a firefighter was the only thing you ever wanted."

"Well, now I want to try something different."

Ryan wore the expression of someone who'd been

goaded by his father one time too many, and she suspected she'd better intervene, little though she wanted to get between two such bullheaded men.

She grasped Joe's arm. "You asked me what I thought about it." She wouldn't look at Ryan when she said this, for fear of giving too much away. "I think Ryan can be a success at whatever he decides to do. And I think you'll be proud of him, no matter what that is."

Joe looked startled and speechless for a moment. He flushed, and she was afraid he was going to explode at her, but he didn't.

"Well, of course I'll be proud of him. I already am proud of him. Ryan knows that."

Judging by Ryan's expression, he hadn't been so sure.

Before he could speak, his mother swept down on them. "The two of you are blocking the buffet table and monopolizing the hostess. You ought to have better sense." She seized a tray. "Either help or get out of the way."

"Out of the way," Joe said quickly. He nudged Ryan. "Show me the plastering job you boys did." They moved off, apparently amicably.

Siobhan smiled, watching them. "I'm sorry about that. When Joe gets something in his head, it takes a bulldozer to get it back out again."

"I didn't want to interfere."

Siobhan squeezed her hand. "Thank you, Laura. You handled him just right."

She headed into the kitchen with the meat-and-cheese tray, and Laura picked up the sadly depleted crab-puff plate and followed her.

"I wasn't really trying to handle him. I just said what I think."

"Well, it was the right thing." Siobhan's fingers moved quickly over the tray, arranging alternating slices of ham and chicken. "Will you do me a favor?"

Laura glanced up at the seriousness of her tone. "Of course, if I can."

"Don't walk out of our lives once the house is sold. We're fond of you and Mandy. We don't want to lose you."

"Thank you, Siobhan. I appreciate that more than I can say. I'm not sure what we'll do or where we'll go after Mandy's surgery."

She blinked back the tears that seemed too near the surface lately. Much as she enjoyed her friendship with the Flanagan family, she didn't think she could go on being close to Ryan, feeling as she did.

"Oh, I know your life might change." Siobhan tucked a sprig of parsley under a cherry tomato. "That keeps happening to people. Look how much Ryan's changed lately. Taking on a new job, new responsibilities—there were times when we never thought that boy would grow up, but he continues to surprise us. Even a charmer like Ryan can be serious when he wants it enough."

She gave Siobhan a sharp look. Was Ryan's mother implying what it sounded like—that Ryan would or could change his negative attitude about being responsible for someone else's happiness?

If so, Siobhan didn't know her son as well as she thought she did. Ryan had made his feelings clear

without saying anything directly, and she had no choice
but to respect that. No matter how much her heart
might ache.

Chapter Twelve

"Sounds like you have quite a defender in Laura." Seth propped his elbow on the bookcase and looked as if he were settling in for a long chat.

The last thing Ryan needed or wanted at the moment was some big brother advice. "I don't know what you're talking about." He accompanied the words with a glare.

Seth didn't seem impressed. "She made Dad back down when he was riding you about the new job. I'd say that's quite an accomplishment."

"I can handle Dad myself."

"Yeah, right." Seth grinned. "Like anyone but Mom has ever been able to do that. I don't know why that should make you act like you've stepped on a hot coal. Laura was being a friend, wasn't she?"

Maybe that was the problem. His friendship with Laura was in rocky enough shape without any further complications.

Mandy ran up to him, arms outstretched for a hug, and saved him from trying to find an answer. She darted off again, chasing Seth's Davy. The laughter in her face touched him. Mandy was opening up.

"That little girl is getting attached to you." Seth's observation carried a faint tone of caution.

"She's a sweet kid. I've been around lately, helping with the house. That's all." Somehow he didn't think Seth was going to buy that.

"You don't need to get defensive about it. I just don't want to see anyone get hurt."

"Do you think I do?" He glared at his brother. "Look, Seth, it's none of your business."

That was one protest too many. He knew it as soon as he said it. Seth would take those words as a challenge, and he wouldn't give up on the subject until he'd delivered some big brotherly advice.

But Seth just studied his face for a long moment. "I see. You're getting attached to Mandy, too. And to Laura."

"What if I am?"

"You tell me."

Usually a good argument with one of his brothers would cheer him up. Not this time. Not when he already knew he was in trouble.

"I didn't mean for this to happen. Hey, you know me. I'm not ready for a serious relationship."

He expected Seth to agree with him. Instead he just smiled.

"Sometimes love happens to you whether you're ready or not."

"Not love." He shied away from the word with a sense of panic. "Just—well, more attached than I meant to be. And now the investigation—"

He stopped.

Seth raised an eyebrow. "What investigation? The fire on the back porch?"

"Yes." He didn't intend to say more, but he couldn't seem to stop himself. Anyway, Seth was safe. "North got another anonymous call. This time the caller said more." He took a breath, hating this. "He said that Laura started the fire herself."

Seth let out his breath in a soundless whistle. "Do you believe that?"

"No. Not a chance in the world. She wouldn't do anything to put her child in danger." He was as sure of that as he was anything in this life.

"I guess someone could argue that she didn't realize the fire would take off so fast. And she was on her way out with Mandy when you got there."

"You sound like North."

"Does he think she did it?" Seth's voice sharpened.

"Who knows what North thinks? He doesn't confide in me. Just tells me to use my brains and work the facts."

He wouldn't add that North frequently looked at him as if doubting he had any brains. That didn't do much for his hope of ever succeeding at this job.

Seth glanced across the room to where Laura stood in conversation with their mother. "Does Laura know about the anonymous tip?"

"No."

"What are you going to do about it?" Seth's tone was carefully neutral, as if to avoid the slightest hint of prejudice either way.

If this situation weren't so serious, he'd almost want to smile. "Don't you want to give me some big brotherly advice?"

Seth didn't move for a moment. Then he grasped his shoulder in a quick, hard grip. "You'll do the right thing. I know."

He blinked. That was a first—a vote of confidence in his judgment from his big brother.

The problem was figuring out what the right thing was.

"Did you two get enough to eat?"

He hadn't heard Laura approach, and he started guiltily at the question.

"I don't know about Ryan, but I'm stuffed." Seth slapped his shoulder. "And I think I'd better stop Davy before he grabs another cupcake."

Seth moved off quickly, leaving him alone with Laura. He cleared his throat, wanting to say—what? There was nothing he could say.

"It's a nice party." Could he have come up with anything more banal if he'd thought about it for a week? Probably not.

Fortunately Laura didn't seem to sense anything wrong.

"It is, isn't it?" She glanced around the room, looking pleased and satisfied. "My first and last here, I guess."

"You have good reason to celebrate." At least, as far

as Laura was concerned, she did. She didn't know that another trouble was looming over her.

"I'd celebrate even more if I were able to get a few last things done before I discuss a contract with my buyer." She glanced at him with a question in her eyes. "Do you have any idea when the arson investigation will be wrapped up?"

He could only hope his face didn't give anything away. "I'm not sure. Why?"

"The insurance company won't pay for the damage to the back porch until the investigation is over."

"I see." He was conscious of treading very carefully. "I didn't realize you were waiting for the insurance company to pay you."

"Well, that's why I have insurance, after all. I can understand why they have to be cautious, but I'd like to have it settled. If my buyer and I go to contract before that, I'll probably need to put the money in an escrow account to cover the damage."

Luckily she couldn't see how fast his mind was racing. "I wish I knew how fast it will go, but I don't. What company are you dealing with?"

She looked at him a little oddly, as if the question hadn't sounded quite right. "Union Casualty. We didn't exactly agree to begin with on what the building was worth, but we settled on a hundred thousand. Now that it's renovated, the new owner will naturally want to reinsure for more."

One hundred thousand. Maybe it wasn't a lot, as city real estate went, but it would more than cover the cost of Mandy's surgery. He didn't like the direction his thoughts were heading, but he couldn't help it. Maybe North's suspicious nature was rubbing off on him.

"Union Casualty's a reputable outfit." He tried to sound as if he had only a casual interest. "I'm sure they'll come through for you."

Once the arson investigation was settled, and depending upon how it was settled.

He didn't believe she had started the fire. He couldn't believe that.

But the insurance, and the need to pay for Mandy's surgery, gave Laura what most investigators would consider a big enough motive for arson.

The sound of the doorbell brought Laura hurrying down the stairs the morning after her party. If that was the missing contractor, finally showing up, she'd like to give him a piece of her mind.

She wouldn't, though. She couldn't afford the luxury of offending him, not until he'd finished the project, at any rate.

She flung the door open before the bell could peal again. But it wasn't the contractor. Ryan stood there, along with the senior arson investigator. What was his name? North, that was it.

"Good morning, Lieutenant North." She glanced at Ryan. He stood a pace behind the other man on the stoop, as if to give North the lead.

"Ms. McKay." North smiled, but his eyes were watchful. "May we come in for a few minutes? There are some things I'd like to go over with you about the fire."

"Of course." She gave a fleeting thought to the window cleaning that had been her project for the morning. "Come upstairs, won't you?"

North glanced into the finished front room as they headed for the steps. "Looks very nice. You've certainly accomplished a great deal here."

"It's coming along." Somehow it seemed inappropriate to comment on how much help Ryan had been. The man was his boss, after all.

She led the way into the living room. "Sit down, please."

"Mandy isn't here?" Ryan spoke for the first time.

"She's spending the day with Nolie." She hesitated, unsure whether she should explain further to North. But why would he care where her daughter was?

She sat down in the rocker, expecting the men to take the sofa, but North pulled over one of the straight chairs from the table instead, bringing it to face her. Something seemed discordant about the gesture, as if he wanted her to know that this wasn't a social call.

All right, fine. She sat up a little straighter. "You wanted to ask me something?"

He shrugged. "Nothing too important. Just a few things that have come up in our investigation we thought you might help us with."

We. She glanced toward Ryan. He wasn't looking at her. Instead he'd pulled out a notebook and was jotting something down. Something cold and hard touched her nerves.

"You made a quick recovery from the fire." North

sounded as if he were making an effort to be casual. "You were lucky it wasn't worse."

"Yes. Thanks to the fire department."

And you, Ryan. Why aren't you looking at me? The room that had been such a cheerful place the night before, filled with friends and laughter, now seemed to have become a battleground.

"Funny thing about that." North's eyes didn't hold any amusement. "We checked out the accelerant. Turns out it was paint thinner. Same as we found in your cellar."

She almost said she'd known that. But probably Ryan shouldn't have told her that.

"The paint thinner I had was in the cellar and the outside door was locked," she said carefully. "No one could have gotten at it."

"Only someone inside the house," he observed.

Someone like you. He didn't say the words, but he didn't need to. For a moment the room swirled around her. He was hinting that she'd started the fire herself.

"None of mine was missing," she said, as if she didn't grasp the implication. "It couldn't have been used to start the fire. And certainly the can of paint thinner that I found later in the alley wasn't mine."

"Yes, that's what you told us." Doubt threaded his words.

"It's true." She looked from the suspicion in North's face to Ryan. Ryan would believe her. But Ryan wasn't looking at her. Wasn't defending her.

A spasm of pain clutched her heart. She fought her

way free of it. She couldn't let herself be weakened by Ryan's defection, not now. Not when she needed every ounce of strength and wit to defend herself.

She faced North. He was her adversary now. "You act as if you think I started the fire myself. Surely you can't believe I'd be so stupid as to start a fire when my daughter and I were on the second floor."

He leaned forward, hands on knees. "You might not have realized the fire would spread as fast as it did. You'd be surprised at the mistakes amateur arsonists make."

Her breath caught, and she had to fight to keep her voice steady. "I'm not an arsonist, amateur or otherwise. This building is all I own. Why on earth would I want to damage it?"

"People will do a lot for a hundred thousand in insurance money, Ms. McKay." His voice was as smooth as silk. "You might have wanted the money more than you wanted the building. It would have paid for your daughter's surgery with enough left over to give you a fresh start."

For a long moment she was speechless. She didn't look toward Ryan, because she couldn't.

No wonder he didn't want to meet her eyes. No wonder he hadn't defended her from North's accusations. He was the source of them.

He had betrayed her.

Laura had been numb when Ryan and North finally left. Maybe that had been a good thing. By the time she was getting Mandy ready for bed, the numbness had worn off, to be replaced by pain so sharp it was all she could do to concentrate on the next step.

Yes, numbness had definitely been better. She watched Mandy pull the pajama top over her head and managed a smile at her success.

North had asked question after question, never verging into rudeness, but always pointed and persistent. He'd circled around and around the subject of the fire, phrasing the same question in a dozen different ways.

Hoping to trip her up, of course. The only reason he hadn't was because she'd been telling the truth. It would have been impossible to construct a lie and maintain it under that relentless questioning.

And all the while, Ryan had sat silent, taking notes. Not looking at her.

Perhaps that had been the thing that hurt the most. Ryan had never met her eyes, even while North used the information he had given to accuse her.

She bent to tuck the covers around Mandy, consciously trying to block that thought out of her mind. If she let herself dwell on how Ryan had betrayed her, she might fall apart entirely.

She couldn't. She had to help Mandy prepare for her hospital stay.

The storybook she'd bought lay on the bed, its colorful cover showing a little badger in a hospital bed. She picked it up. "Do you want a story?"

Mandy shook her head, and her fingers moved. *Nolie said she'd come and see me in the hospital. She said she'd say a prayer for me.*

"That's good, darling." Tears stung her eyes. What

kind of friendship could she have with any of the Flanagans now?

Can we say a prayer about going to the hospital?

For an instant she didn't know if she could do that. Then she managed to nod. "Do you want to say it?"

Mandy nodded. Her hands moved.

Jesus, help me not to be scared when I go to the hospital. And help Mommy not to be scared, either.

"Amen," Laura whispered the word, signing it. *Amen.*

Mandy slid down into her bed, smiling. She snuggled her teddy bear against her face. *Tomorrow I'll get my new bear. Ryan will bring it to the hospital.*

Her throat tightened. How did she explain Ryan's defection to Mandy? What she'd feared all along had come to pass—Mandy had learned to love him, and he'd let them down.

"We'll see." She struggled to smile. "Night-night, sweetheart." She kissed Mandy's cheek, adjusted the nightlight, and got out of the room before her tears could spill over.

She sank down on the sofa, wiping her wet cheeks, swallowing her sobs. If she once gave way to them, she might fall apart entirely. She had to be strong for what tomorrow would bring.

Tomorrow. Mandy thought Ryan would come to the hospital, as he'd promised. She knew better.

She leaned back against the sofa, utterly spent, her throat choked with unshed tears. North had demanded that she come to department headquarters tomorrow to make a formal statement. Only the fact of Mandy's surgery had let her postpone it until Friday.

Friday, when her buyer was due to arrive. How would all of this affect her sale? Could she sell the property if she were under arrest for arson? Maybe she should be talking to an attorney.

The doorbell rang. She pushed herself slowly to her feet. It could be anyone, but she knew who it would be. If she didn't go down, he'd stand there ringing the bell until she couldn't stand it any longer.

A wave of anger, hot and strong, swept through her. Stiffening her spine, she stalked down the steps and flung the door open.

"What do you want now? Do you have more questions?"

She'd expect Ryan to step back at the heat of her anger, but he just stood there, looking at her steadily.

"No. No more questions. May I come in?"

She stepped back, letting him enter, but switched on the light in the downstairs room. "We won't go upstairs. I just put Mandy to bed, and I don't want her disturbed."

And I don't want you in my living room again, Ryan, because it might make me remember when you kissed me.

"That's all right." He closed the door. "I won't be long. I probably shouldn't be here, but I couldn't stay away."

"How am I supposed to react to that? Should I be happy to see you after what you've done?"

"Laura—"

"No." She took another step away from him, holding out her hands as if he'd tried to approach her. "Don't bother telling me you're sorry. I talked to you as a friend, and you carried everything I said straight to your boss."

"Laura, I am sorry. But I didn't have any choice."

"We always have choices. You just chose your job."

"It is my job." He looked stung. "It's my duty. Can't you understand that the only way through this investigation is to bring out the truth?"

"What truth? You and North just want to settle for the easy answer. I have insurance on the property and I need money, so I must be guilty."

"No." That almost sounded like pain in his voice, and there was no laughter in his face now. "We're not looking for easy answers, but you can't expect me to ignore what you told me. Face it, Laura. It gives you a motive. I can't pretend that isn't so because we're friends."

Friends. She once hoped they'd be more. Now she knew they couldn't even be that.

Her throat tightened. She couldn't go on looking at him, listening to his voice. She had to get him out of there.

"You'd better leave. You want me to make you feel better about what you did, and I can't. So just go."

He stiffened, fingers clenching into fists. "I'm not looking for forgiveness. I just want you to understand."

"I understand. You let us rely on you, and you let us down." Why was she surprised? Wasn't that what always happened?

His face was a mask, with only those blazing blue eyes to say a living person was behind it. "I guess there's nothing I can say to that. At least take my advice and get an attorney. Don't make a formal statement without one."

"Aren't you afraid you're compromising your job by telling me that?"

He didn't react to the jab. "There's someone the family uses that I can recommend, if—"

"No." She pushed the suggestion away with both hands. "I'll find my own attorney. You should be happy about that. I won't involve you."

"I am involved. I can't help but be. We're—"

"Don't say we're friends. We're not." She wrapped her arms around herself to still the shaking that had begun deep inside.

"I can't walk away that easily."

"Do you believe I'm guilty?" She threw the question at him.

"No." His response snapped back. "I know you're not."

"That makes it worse, not better." She shook her head. "You like to pretend you're not good at responsibility, but that's not it. You're afraid. You may be fearless in a burning building, but you're terrified of emotional involvement. Well, congratulations, Ryan. You found the perfect way out."

She yanked the door open. "Goodbye. Please don't come back. Ever."

Chapter Thirteen

She'd pulled the vinyl chair as close to the hospital bed as she could, but it still wasn't close enough. Laura put her hand over Mandy's, as much to reassure herself as to reassure her child.

Her daughter gave her a quick smile and turned her attention back to the cartoon characters on the television screen. Mandy had been taken by the novelty of having her very own television that she could watch in bed. She had happily settled back against the pillows, not even objecting when she had to put on the hospital's cotton printed gown instead of her own pajamas.

Laura fought to keep her smile on straight as she glanced at her watch. She'd thought the procedure would be over by now, but it was afternoon already and still they hadn't begun Mandy's sedation. Dr. Phillips had popped in earlier with an apologetic smile. An emergency required his attention, and Mandy's procedure would be delayed.

Clearly that bothered Laura more than it did Mandy. Her daughter seemed unconcerned, dividing her attention among coloring books, television cartoons and her teddy, who sat propped against the bed railing.

Was Mandy's calm due to those prayers they'd shared the previous night? She couldn't be sure, but whatever had caused it, she was thankful. Surely God had listened to Mandy's prayers.

The thought startled her. Was she beginning to fumble her way back to a relationship with God? If so, her friendship with the Flanagan family was responsible for that, and she didn't know whether to be glad or sorry.

She pressed her palms together, willing herself to be still. If she got up and paced or did anything else to show her stress, Mandy would pick up on it.

The memory of Ryan's visit certainly didn't do anything to give her peace. Just thinking about it tightened her throat and squeezed her heart.

She'd been harsh with him, but he'd deserved it. He hadn't even admitted he was in the wrong or said he was sorry for what he'd done. He'd just expected her to understand he'd acted out of some concept of duty.

Well, she didn't. She fought to harden her heart against the pain. Ryan had gone, and she was on her own again. That was okay. She was used to that. She didn't need Ryan or any of his family.

But just at this moment, waiting for Mandy's surgery, she wouldn't have minded a little company.

The swinging door creaked, as if in answer to her

thought. Nolie peeked around the door's edge, her smile encompassing both of them.

"Hi, how are you?" Her hands moved with her words. "May I come in?"

"Of course." Laura rose as Mandy held out both arms to Nolie, then she stepped back so Nolie could reach the bed. "As you can see, we're waiting out a delay."

"We heard." Brendan came in behind Nolie. He looked oddly formal in the clerical collar he no doubt wore for hospital visits, but his smile was warm and the grasp of his hand comforting. "I checked early this morning to see when we ought to come."

"Siobhan wants to visit, too, but we decided to take turns." Nolie settled onto the hospital bed, handing Mandy a gift bag. "She'll stop by later."

"She—you didn't need to." Ridiculous, that her throat was choked by their simple act of caring.

"We want to be here." Brendan squeezed her hand and then went to the bed to ruffle Mandy's hair. "How are you doing, Mandy?"

She was too busy pulling tissue paper out of the gift bag to answer, but that didn't matter. Her expression when she pulled a fluffy, black-and-white stuffed puppy from the bag more than made up for it.

She hugged the stuffed animal close, burying her face in its fur.

"I thought you'd like it." Nolie's voice sounded a little choked.

"She's going to have you accepting one of those puppies whether you want it or not," Brendan murmured. "Better watch out."

"It might be worth it, to see Mandy that happy."

She couldn't believe she was saying that. Probably she was lightheaded. She hadn't realized how tense she was until their presence chased her fears away, at least for the moment.

Did they know about the investigation? About the breach between her and Ryan?

Her tension came flooding back. If so, they'd be on Ryan's side. The Flanagans always stuck together—everyone knew that.

She didn't want their comfort under false pretenses. "I don't know if Ryan told you—"

Brendan cut off the words with a quick squeeze of her hand. "We know about the investigation. Lieutenant North is crazy if he thinks you had anything to do with starting the fire. We're all sure of that."

"Thank you." Her throat tightened at the sureness in his voice, and she had to force the words out. "I appreciate the vote of confidence."

They probably still thought Ryan had done the right thing in telling North about her insurance, but at this moment, she didn't care. They believed in her and they were here, that was all that mattered.

Brendan pulled another chair over, so that they sat in a semi-circle close to Mandy. Brendan reached out to clasp her hand.

"Shall we pray?"

She managed a nod. She wouldn't reject prayers on Mandy's behalf.

"Father, you know why we're here today." Brendan's tone was relaxed and conversational, and Nolie's smile was warm as she translated his words. "We ask You to be with Mandy and her doctors and help her to get well quickly. We all love her. Amen."

"Amen." Laura's voice trembled a little, and she fought to steady it.

Maybe it was fortunate that the nurse bustled in just then. Otherwise she might have let a tear escape.

"Sorry to interrupt, but it's time for this little lady to have something to make her sleepy. They'll be ready for her soon."

Laura's tension spiked again as she moved back from the bed to give the nurse room. Brendan slid his chair back against the wall.

"Maybe we'd better slip out for the moment," he said. "I have a few other people to visit, but I'll come back afterward, if that's okay."

She nodded. She wouldn't have asked him, but it would be good to have someone there while she waited. It wasn't Brendan's fault that he wasn't the right Flanagan.

Was she crazy, longing for Ryan's presence even when he'd let her down so badly?

"I have to go, too." Nolie leaned over to hug Laura and then patted her bulging tummy. "Doctor's appointment. I hope she'll say this baby is coming soon."

"Good luck." Laura let her hand rest on Nolie's, remembering the feeling of carrying a child, knowing your life was about to change irrevocably. Would she ever feel that again? It seemed unlikely. "And thank you for coming."

"How could I not?" Nolie smiled and waved at

Mandy. "And don't forget, one of those puppies is ear-marked for you."

Laura didn't bother protesting, knowing Nolie was just trying to lighten her mood. Nolie understood. They could be good friends, if not for the fact that she was Ryan's sister-in-law. If Ryan helped prosecute her for arson, no friendship was likely to survive that.

She kept coming back to that, no matter how hard she tried to push it out of her mind. If Ryan—

The door opened, and Ryan came in.

For a moment she couldn't speak. Brendan and Nolie, probably sensing the tension, exchanged glances. Then they slipped out the door behind him.

She finally found her voice. "What are you doing here?"

"I promised Mandy I'd come." Both his face and his voice were tight. He held up a teddy bear dressed in a firefighter's costume. "Believe it or not, I keep my promises."

For a moment Ryan thought Laura would push him right out the door, teddy bear and all. Then she stepped back, and he caught sight of Mandy, her figure incredibly small in the high, white hospital bed.

She lay back against the pillows. Her eyes drooped, but she gave him a sweet smile. That smile reached right into his chest and squeezed his heart until he couldn't breathe.

This must be how Seth had felt when his little boy was sick—helpless, desperate, ready to change places in an instant if he could.

Mandy wasn't his child. She would never be his child. But still, the feelings were there.

He went to her bedside, holding out the teddy bear. "See? I told you I'd bring you Firefighter Teddy to keep you company while you're in the hospital."

Mandy smiled sleepily. She held out her arms—not for the teddy bear, but for him.

He bent to hug her, feeling her small arms tight around his neck. And his heart.

Laura's accusation the previous night slid out from the hiding place where'd he'd locked it.

You're terrified of emotional involvement, Ryan. Well, congratulations. You've found the perfect way out.

That wasn't true. It wasn't.

He slammed the thought back behind doors and concentrated on Mandy. That wasn't easy, but it was easier than looking at Laura and seeing the pain in her eyes.

"You're sleepy, aren't you?" He brushed dark curls back from Mandy's face.

She nodded. I knew you'd come. Her fingers signed the words slowly.

If so, she'd known more than he had. North had told him he should steer clear of Laura and her child, but he couldn't do it. Not today, not when he'd promised to be here.

"You need to go to sleep now, sweetheart. I'll leave you with Mommy."

She grabbed his hand, stopping him when he would have moved away. Come back. Promise.

He could feel Laura's tension, even without looking at her. But this wasn't about him and Laura. It was about Mandy's needs.

"I'll come back. I promise."

She nodded, face relaxing. Her eyes flickered shut.

He turned toward Laura, but before she could say any of the things she undoubtedly had stored up to blast him with, a nurse and an orderly came in, pushing a gurney.

"Time to go," the woman said quietly.

He stepped out of their way. He ought to leave them alone, but one look at Laura stopped him. She bent over the bed, helping to move Mandy to the gurney. She even managed a smile as she bent over to give her daughter a kiss. But he could feel her pain as if it were his own.

"I'll be right here waiting when you come back," she whispered.

Mandy's breath was even, her eyes closed. She didn't hear the words, but no doubt it comforted Laura to say them.

The nurse nodded, and they wheeled the cart smoothly out the door.

Laura took a step after them, reaching out as if she couldn't help herself. The door swung shut. She turned, walked back to the empty bed and stood there, her hands clasping the railing.

His heart was a heavy weight in his chest. He had to help her, but what could he do?

"Laura, let me stay with you. Please."

He knew the answer before she shook her head.

She didn't want him there. He was the one who'd let her down.

All the familiar arguments he'd been rehearsing since the night before flickered through his mind. He was only doing his job. He couldn't help it. He had a duty.

Funny. None of them even convinced him.

"I'll come back." He spun and stalked out of the room, restraining the frustration that made him want to slam the door on its hinges.

"Whoa." Brendan took a step out of his path. "What's eating you?"

He glared at his cousin, glad to have someone to vent his feelings on. "That's obvious, isn't it? Especially to a trained professional like you."

Brendan glanced at the closed door, grabbed his arm, and pulled him the few feet to the end of the hallway. A window looked out over flat roofs.

"It seems like Laura doesn't need to hear this conversation."

"Yeah, you're right." Ryan braced his hands on the windowsill, staring out. A light rain had started, and the black tar roofs glistened with moisture.

Brendan just waited.

Whatever he might say was safe with Brendan. Trouble was, he really didn't know what he was feeling right now, so how could he put it into words?

"Look," he said gruffly, "go in there and stay with Laura until Mandy gets back from surgery, okay? She shouldn't be alone right now."

Brendan didn't move. "Why don't you stay?"

He rolled his shoulders against the tension. "Because she doesn't want me. She thinks I betrayed her confidence. Thinks I'm helping North railroad her."

"Is she right?"

"Not that anyone is railroading her. North's an honest man. But—"

"But North thinks Laura is guilty," Brendan finished for him.

"Who knows what he thinks?" Irritation edged his voice. "The man's like a sphinx. But when I tried to defend Laura, he accused me of losing my objectivity."

"Are you?"

He glared at the rain-wet pane. "Maybe. I can't think straight where Laura's concerned."

"You don't doubt her innocence, do you?"

"Of course not. Laura would never put that little girl in danger. Ever."

He could hear the certainty in his voice. He might not know a lot of things about this case, but he knew that beyond question.

Brendan leaned against the concrete-block wall. "That's my feeling, too, but you know Laura a lot better than I do. Have you told North that?"

"Several times." His mouth twisted in a wry grin. "Several times too many, probably. He's ready to boot me from the squad if I can't 'forget my feelings for the woman.'" He shot a defiant look at his cousin. "And don't ask me what those feelings are. I haven't figured that out yet. I just know she didn't start that fire."

"Then it looks like you have to prove that, whether North wants you to or not."

"Are you telling me to disobey a direct order? Isn't the fire-department chaplain supposed to keep us on the straight and narrow?"

"Sometimes you have to decide for yourself what's right, no matter what the regulations say." Brendan's mouth quirked in a half smile. "But don't you tell your dad I said that."

Ryan almost felt the weight slipping off his shoulders. He had to do what was right. That meant finding the proof that Laura hadn't started that fire.

And if it cost him his job—well, that would be worth it.

He slapped Brendan's shoulder. "Thanks, Bren. I'll be back. Take care of them for me."

He turned and strode down the hall, energy coursing through him. He felt right about what he was doing for the first time in days.

The proof was out there somewhere. No matter what, he had to find it.

A few hours later, Ryan had begun to doubt. Not Laura's innocence—that was never a question in his mind.

No, what he doubted was his own ability to find out the truth. He slammed his hand down on the desk next to the computer keyboard. He'd been through all the reports, all the forensic tests, a half dozen times. Still he wasn't seeing anything new.

Give him a burning building, he knew what to do. With this—

"Having problems?" North leaned over his chair,

scanning the report of the second fire that was displayed on the computer screen. "Why are you going over this one again?"

An evasion leaped to his lips, and he forced it away. He wouldn't try to hide what he was doing from North. He owed the man honesty, at least.

But maybe he didn't have to start with his conviction that Laura was innocent. That was emotion, not fact.

He pointed at the screen. "This doesn't make sense. Not to me, anyway. It almost looks as if the second fire was intended not to cause any damage."

The lines in North's face deepened. "If Ms. McKay started it, she did it to make us think we were chasing an arsonist. She might not have wanted to cause damage."

"If you're trying to make me believe she left her sleeping daughter alone in the house so she could creep through the streets with a gas can and take a chance of being caught, you're going to have to come up with a better reason than that." He let his skepticism show in his voice. "She's not a stupid woman. She'd know what the risks were."

North didn't give any indication that Ryan's argument impressed him, but at least he didn't tell him to shut up. "What's your theory then?"

"I don't have one." He glared at the screen. "If she did it, why was there a second fire? If there really is an arsonist, why hasn't he struck again? And who's making the anonymous calls?"

North's face tightened. "I don't like anonymous

calls. Never have. This caller—it's like he's trying to lead us along a path, dropping bread crumbs leading to Ms. McKay."

"That's how I feel about it." Ryan tried not to sound too eager. For the first time, North was actually listening to him. "If there *was* someone in the alley where she says she found that paint-thinner can, then it looks like someone wants to torch that particular building. Maybe it doesn't have anything to do with a pyro."

North raised his eyebrows. "That theory leads us right back to Ms. McKay. Who else has reason to want that building down? She's the one with insurance on it. Who else would benefit?"

"I don't know." He shoved his chair back. "But I'm not going to find out staring at reports I've already read a dozen times."

"Where are you going?"

"To talk to everyone in the surrounding buildings again. Maybe someone saw something they haven't mentioned. Or maybe we didn't ask the right questions."

North looked at him for a moment, as if weighing him in his mind. Then he nodded.

"All right. We'll open it up again." He put up a hand to forestall any thanks. "But understand this, Flanagan. No matter what either of us feels, if we don't find anything new, the case against Ms. McKay is going to the district attorney's office on Monday."

"We will." Ryan headed for the door.

We have to. Father, are You listening? We have to.

Chapter Fourteen

The waiting was endless. With Mandy no longer in the hospital room, Laura gave in to the impulse to pace.

"It's hard, I know." Brendan's gaze held sympathy. "Waiting for word on your child has to be the most difficult thing in the world."

She nodded, realized her hands were twisting together, and let them drop. "Really, Brendan, you don't need to wait with me. I appreciate it, but I'm sure you have other people who need you."

"There's no place I'd rather be than here right now." He leaned forward, elbows on his knees, hands lightly linked. "Besides, I promised Ryan."

She shot a startled glance at him. "You promised him what?"

"That I'd stay." He said it as comfortably as if the polite barriers between people didn't exist between them. As if they were family. "He felt you didn't want him here, so he asked me to stay. Not that he needed to. I would have, in any event."

"I see." But she didn't see, not really. Was he saying that Ryan, despite what happened, still felt responsible for her?

She was still struggling with that when the door began to swing open. Her heart seemed to catch in her throat. The doctor—

But it was Siobhan, not Dr. Phillips.

Siobhan glanced at Brendan, a question in her eyes. "Still waiting?"

He nodded, glancing at his watch. "From what Laura told me about the procedure, I'd say they'll bring Mandy down from surgery soon."

"It seems like forever, doesn't it?" Siobhan crossed the room and hugged her. "I know. My kids put me through the waiting more than a few times. Especially Ryan. For awhile he had a broken bone every year, it seemed."

Tears spilled over at the warmth of Siobhan's hug, and Laura dashed them away. Silly. She didn't long for her own mother's presence, but somehow Siobhan made her feel like a child being comforted.

"Thank you for coming." She ought to say again that they needn't stay, but she didn't want to. She wanted them here, despite everything that had happened with Ryan.

Siobhan set the oversized purse she carried on the bed and pulled out a thermos. "I brought coffee from home. Nobody should have to drink hospital coffee, especially at a stressful time like this."

She produced mugs and poured, then handed a thick white mug to Laura.

Laura wrapped her fingers around it, feeling the

warmth. Feeling comforted. Amazing, how Siobhan created a sense of home wherever she went.

The door swung open again, and Dr. Phillips strode into the room. Her throat choked, and her heart seemed to stop beating.

His eyes lit at the sight of the coffee. "If that's real coffee, Siobhan, I'll have some."

"First things first," Siobhan said quickly.

Dr. Phillips's lined face relaxed in a smile as he looked at Laura. "There's nothing to worry about—the procedure went perfectly. I've just checked on her again. Mandy's on her way down now, and everything should be fine."

Her legs didn't want to support her, and the coffee sloshed dangerously in the mug. She felt Brendan's arm supporting her as he led her to a chair.

"It's okay, Laura. She's going to be fine. Just take it easy."

By the time the room stopped spinning around, she realized that Siobhan was scolding the doctor as if he were a ten-year-old in her church-school class. He looked rather sheepish as he came to squat next to Laura's chair.

"I'm sorry. I guess Siobhan's right—my bedside manner leaves a little to be desired. Just because the procedure is routine to me doesn't mean it is for you. But I promise, your little girl is perfectly all right."

She grabbed his hand, wanting to believe his words but not quite daring to. "Will it work? Will her hearing be improved?"

"We won't know for sure until we activate the device in a month, of course. But from everything I can see so far, I think the results will be good." He patted her hand. "That's all we can hope for. You know that."

"I know." She started to say that she didn't expect a miracle, but then she realized that wasn't true. It would be a miracle if Mandy were released from her silent world. "Thank God."

"Yes." Brendan patted her shoulder. "Thank God."

She ought to tell him how much she appreciated his prayers and his presence, but just then the gurney rolled through the doorway, and everything else left her mind in her need to reach her daughter.

"Mandy."

She stopped, longing to touch her but not sure where to touch. The side of Mandy's head was bandaged, and tubes extended from her arms.

The doctor had shown her pictures before the surgery. She'd known to expect bruises and swelling. She just hadn't known how she'd feel when it was Mandy.

"She looks so—" Her voice choked.

Siobhan's arm went around her, holding her as they transferred Mandy smoothly to the bed. "I know." Siobhan's voice was soft. "It's so hard to see your child looking like that. To know you made the decision that led to it."

She nodded, unable to speak. How did Siobhan know exactly what she was thinking?

"You did the right thing," Siobhan said firmly. "This was a hard decision, but you did the right thing. The bruises will be quickly forgotten, but the good results will be permanent."

Her mind cleared, the whirl of guilt and fear dissipating. "Yes. You're right." She went to the bed, her hand closing over Mandy's fingers. "She's going to be fine."

Thank you, God.

Siobhan patted her back gently. "I know Ryan wanted to be here."

She shook her head. "Don't. I'm sorry, but please, don't." She couldn't think about Ryan, not now.

Siobhan nodded. "All right. I understand."

If she really understood, it was more than Laura did. She just knew that at this moment, all she could concentrate on was her daughter. Dealing with her feelings for Ryan would have to wait.

It was dark when she pulled up at the townhouse. She parked and then sat, too emotionally exhausted to get out of the car.

Mandy was all right—that was the important thing. She'd wakened, smiled at the sight of her mother, and gone back to sleep. Laura had sat in the chair next to the bed, holding her hand, unwilling to let go.

Dr. Phillips had finally come back into the room to check on Mandy. He'd been kindness itself when he detached her hand from her daughter's. Laura was exhausted, he'd said firmly, and Mandy would undoubtedly sleep through the rest of the night. It was time for her to go home and get some rest.

So she'd come home, but not to rest. How could she, when her mind kept going around and around like a hamster on a wheel? She couldn't turn off the busy thoughts.

She forced herself out of the car. Unlock the door. Too tired to search for the light switch—just climb the stairs. Her feet took them automatically, knowing the way even in the dark.

She glanced at her watch when she reached the living room. She kept a table lamp burning all the time since the fire, and its yellow glow welcomed her. In a few short hours, she'd have to present herself at the fire department headquarters building, where the arson squad was located.

Lieutenant North, with his inimical gaze, would be waiting for her to make a formal statement. Would Ryan be there, too? Her mind winced away from that thought.

And what would come next? Once they had her version of events signed, then what?

Ryan had urged that she get an attorney, but she'd been too preoccupied with Mandy's surgery even to think about that. She should have found the time. Instinct told her it would be unwise to go into that meeting without some professional counsel.

She flipped open the phone book, but the long list of attorneys blurred before her eyes. She rubbed the back of her neck. She'd take care of that tomorrow morning. Brendan would probably be willing to recommend someone.

The red light on her answering machine was blinking. She pressed the button warily, half afraid of what fresh trouble might be waiting for her.

It was the prospective buyer for the building, reminding her that she'd arrive in Suffolk in the morning. Unless she heard otherwise from Laura, she'd come to the townhouse at one in the afternoon. She couldn't wait to see what Laura had accomplished with the place.

Laura looked at her watch again, but it hadn't miraculously decided to give her any more time. Less than fourteen hours, and she'd be showing the house.

If she went to bed, she'd never sleep. Maybe some hard physical labor would ease the stress. She grabbed her bag. She'd given the hospital her cell phone number in case of any emergency. They'd call if Mandy woke and needed her.

She started up the flight of stairs to the third floor, determination driving her, and came out into the open area that was the last thing yet to be finished.

The contractor had let her down, of course. All of his promises had come to nothing, and the partition still stood. She rapped on it, eyeing the sledgehammer that leaned against the wall.

This wasn't a bearing wall—just a flimsy partition. She'd do what she should have done before this and knock it out herself. She wouldn't have time to frame in the opening, but at least Ms. Jamison could visualize the workroom she could put in here.

The woman would love it. She wouldn't have taken an option on the place if she hadn't been able to picture how perfect it would be for her business. One of the last remaining available buildings in the historic district—she'd jump at the chance to close the deal.

Laura grabbed the sledgehammer. It was heavier than she'd thought, or maybe she was just more tired.

She had to drag it across the floor to the offending partition.

Would she be able to close the deal if she were arrested for arson? What would happen to Mandy if something like that happened to her?

Her stomach churned. She'd begun to believe she could count on Ryan. She'd actually thought—

Well, that didn't matter any longer. Loving him had been a mistake, but at least it had shown her that she was capable of loving someone again.

Maybe, someday, her heart would no longer splinter at the thought of him. She'd be able to move on.

Tears blurred her vision as she hefted the sledgehammer and swung it at the wall. It connected with a satisfying thud, penetrating the plaster and shattering the lath beneath.

Something rumbled and cracked. She looked up, startled, but it was too late. Before she could move, the whole wall came down on her in a flood of plaster and bricks, knocking her to the floor, burying her.

She struggled, choking on thick dust, trying to see, to understand what happened. Dazed, she put her hand to her head, feeling a lump. Had she been knocked out?

If so, it hadn't been long. Plaster dust still swirled in the air. She was flat on her back, debris on top of her, staring up at the ceiling.

Slowly her brain began to made sense of what she was seeing. The flimsy partition had filled in an archway, masking the old wall of brick and mortar that went the rest of the way to the ceiling.

She must have hit the supporting pillar of the arch with that careless blow. It had collapsed, bringing down the heavier structure above the partition, far more than she expected.

Stupid. Her father would never have made a mistake like that. She'd overestimated her own abilities, and now she was paying the price.

She raised her head, letting out an involuntary groan. She had a splitting headache, but her exploring fingers didn't find any blood. All right. She wasn't hurt, and everything could be fixed, cleaned up, made like new. All she had to do was get up and do it.

She couldn't. She tried to get up, and she couldn't move. Panic ripped through her, and she struggled against the debris, arms flailing wildly as she tried to shove it away.

All she succeeded in doing was stirring up the dust. It lifted into the air, wrapping around her, filling her eyes and ears and mouth. Coughing and choking, she fell back.

An eternity later, she opened her eyes again. This couldn't be happening to her.

Why are You letting this happen to me?

She couldn't be trapped in her own house, not when Mandy needed her. Mandy. The hospital.

The thought of her daughter seemed to steady her. She took a cautious breath. The dust had settled again. Calmly, quietly, she had to assess the situation.

Trying not to think beyond the next moment, she attempted to move one part of her body at a time. Something had hit her in the head, obviously, but it didn't seem too bad. Her arms moved, free of the debris. Her ribs—she winced. Her ribs hurt, but she didn't think anything was broken. Her legs—

Her legs were trapped. Cautiously she flexed the muscles and wiggled her toes. Nothing hurt. She pushed herself up onto her elbows so that she could see what was going on.

The rough-hewn beam that had supported the archway lay diagonally across her legs. Four-by-four, at least, and it must weigh a ton. Thankfully it had fallen so that it wedged against the opposite wall, keeping that deadly weight off her body.

She wasn't hurt. She was just trapped.

The wave of panic came again, the primitive terror of being trapped and helpless. She fought it down. She wouldn't get out of this by letting herself panic. She had to think.

Maybe, if she moved very carefully, she could wiggle her way out. Bracing her hands against the rubble, she pushed her body backward. Nothing.

Biting her lip, she fought down the fear. If she could shift some of the rubble from underneath her, it might give her a precious inch or two. That would be enough.

She pulled at the scraps of plaster and lath, clawing debris out from under her with her fingers. It was slow, terribly slow, with nowhere to put the pieces she dragged out. She tried piling them up, but they kept sliding down over her arm.

Her finger caught on a projecting nail. She pulled the board free, careful not to cut herself again, and thrust it away from her. She sucked at her finger. She'd need a tetanus booster when she got out of here.

Finally she felt nothing but floorboards under her. Now. Bracing her hands again, she pushed away from the heavy beam. Her legs slid an inch, then another. She was doing it, she was going to get out—

With an ominous creak, the beam shifted. She froze. It was going to come down on her—

Please, God, please, God.

The beam settled, sending up another cloud of plaster dust.

She coughed, her throat raw. It hadn't crushed her legs. It had just settled more firmly in place. She couldn't get out unless someone lifted the beam away from her.

Why aren't You helping me?

Tears stung her eyes. Had she drifted so far from God that He no longer heard her?

My mother would say…that we are God's hands on earth, put here to help each other.

Ryan had said that, or something close to it. His words had stuck like a burr in her mind, refusing to be dismissed or forgotten.

God sent other people to do His work. To help her. Ryan. His friends. The people from the church, the rest of the Flanagan family. In her blindness, she hadn't seen God at work in their readiness to help her.

Instead, trapped by her pride and independence, she rejected people.

Not entirely. She pressed her palms against her eyes, seeing faces against the blackness there. She'd begun, once Ryan came back into her life, to move out of her isolation, but each time something went wrong, she'd retreated. It had seemed safer, somehow, to stay trapped rather than risk being hurt yet again.

She'd been trapped spiritually. Now she was trapped physically, and Mandy was alone.

The panic came again, and she moved recklessly. The beam creaked and settled, and now she began to feel its weight, pressing down. She could visualize bones crumbling under that weight.

Help me, please, Father. I've been wrong. I haven't trusted You. I've blamed You. Forgive me. Help me now, for Mandy's sake if not my own. I can't do it myself any longer. I need You.

Her tears spilled over, bitter at first, and then gradually healing, as if they washed away all the pride, all the isolation, all the pain.

At last she lay silent, peace seeping through her. It replaced the panic and cleared her mind, and with it came a sense of God's presence that was so strong she knew she would never be alone again.

Show me the way, Father. I can't find it on my own.

She raised her head, realizing that she could assess the situation without panic. She was still trapped. She couldn't free herself. Maybe she could find a way to get help.

If she managed to throw something through the window, would someone on the street below notice? She scrabbled through the debris, searching for a piece small enough and heavy enough to break the window.

Her fingers closed on a piece of brick. Hefting it, she swung her arm back as far as possible and threw it toward the closest window. It hit the wall and bounced harmlessly to the floor.

She never had been very good at baseball. She brushed through the rubble, searching for another brick. Nothing but fragments of plaster met her fingers.

Her searching fingers disturbed a pile of debris. It slid away from her, exposing a thin strip of leather. Her handbag, with the cell phone inside!

If she could reach it—she strained, fingers stretching, and then sank back. Not even close. But if she could snag the leather strap with something, maybe she could pull it toward her.

There, staring her in the face, was just what she needed—the board with the exposed nail that had cut her finger. *Thank You, Lord.* She grasped the end of the board, extending it toward the handbag strap.

It reached. Excitement flooded through her, and she struggled for calm. Easy, easy, she had to be careful, she couldn't risk losing the strap or pushing it farther away with a sudden motion.

She edged the board a cautious inch at a time, her muscles straining to hold it steady. *Please, Father.* Her prayers seemed to keep time with the thudding of her heart.

At last the nail slid under the strap. She turned the board until it snagged and began to pull. Careful, careful. Don't let it slip away.

Another inch. Two. The rest of the debris slid away, exposing the bag, still closed. Inch by precious inch she pulled the bag toward her. Finally she could grasp it in her hands.

She fumbled with the latch, murmuring prayers of thanksgiving. Her fingers closed around the cool plastic of the phone, and she pulled it free.

The digital display was beautiful, just beautiful, showing her the phone was working. It could so easily have been smashed by the falling debris, but it hadn't been. It was there, waiting for her, her lifeline.

Thank You, Father. Her tears spilled over again. *Thank You.*

She could call 911, but she wanted someone else. She punched in a number she hadn't even realized she had memorized—of Ryan's cell phone.

Chapter Fifteen

Ryan had done this a hundred times before on the job. Why was he all thumbs now?

He knew the answer to that. Because it was Laura who was trapped, Laura who needed him.

Ryan forced himself to focus on nothing but the screwdriver in his hand and the lock on the front door of the townhouse. *Think,* breathe, don't let yourself be distracted by the need to reach her now.

She'd said she was okay. She was stuck, trapped, but not injured. Her voice on the cell phone had sounded remarkably calm.

He wasn't. His professional detachment had deserted him completely. *Let her be all right, Lord. Keep her safe.*

The lock popped. He yanked open the door and raced up the stairs, adrenaline pumping. He always loved that adrenaline rush, pouring through him, making him feel as if he could move mountains.

Not now. Not when it was Laura. His heart pounded against his ribs, running wild at the thought of her.

He passed the living-room door on the second floor and thundered on up the stairs to the third floor. "Laura! Are you okay?"

He surged onto the third-floor level and stopped. The adrenaline still demanded action, but long years of training began to take over.

Stop. Assess the situation. Don't do anything to make it worse.

The floor was littered with bricks and plaster, and the partition Laura had planned to remove was nothing but a jagged hole. Laura lay, propped on her elbows, dust-covered and disheveled, underneath a mass of rubble on the floor. But she smiled at him.

"A mess, isn't it?" Her tone was quiet, almost conversational, as if she came this close to disaster every day and it didn't bother her.

"Pretty much." He managed a smile. Keep her talking, assess her injuries, figure out a safe way to remove her from danger.

"I tried to take the wall down myself." She grimaced. "Pretty stupid, huh?"

"Just a bit." He circled her, checking out the situation. Most of the debris was small stuff, easily moved, but the beam that had fallen across her was another matter. "Does anything hurt?"

"Not bad. Bumps and bruises, I think. I'm sure nothing's broken."

He circled the beam carefully and then squatted next to her. "Are you sure? Can you feel your legs?"

Her smile reassured him. "Yes, they're fine." The smile trembled. "I'm glad to see you."

He let himself touch her cheek. "Me, too. When I got your call—"

No, he'd better not go on with how that had made him feel, or he might lose it entirely. Laura needed his professional skill right now.

"You couldn't have been far away. You got here in minutes."

She didn't know how close he'd been. He'd actually forgotten about what he'd been doing when she called. He cleared his throat.

"I called the station. The paramedics are on their way right now."

She put her hand over his, pressing it against her cheek. "I'm fine. I don't need paramedics—I just need to get out of here." Emotion darkened her eyes. "Mandy could be waking up. I have to get back to the hospital."

"Right." That was another thing he'd forgotten about in his need to know that Laura was safe. "But we should wait for them. The paramedic team will have the equipment to get you out safely."

Her hand tightened on his. "Please, Ryan. Can't you break the rules just this once? If you can lift the beam, I'm sure I can slide out."

He leaned forward, balancing himself carefully with one hand pressed against the floor. The beam was wedged against the wall on one side—that was the only thing that had saved Laura from injury. He ought to be able to lift it enough to release her.

He shouldn't. She wasn't in imminent danger, so he

should wait for back-up. But Laura was looking at him with confidence shining in her dark eyes, and he gave in to the need to have her safe.

"Okay. I've broken plenty of rules already today. I guess one more won't hurt."

He got into position, bracing the rough beam with his shoulder. "If anything hurts when you try to move, you stop right away, okay? We're not taking any chances of making things worse."

She nodded. "You're the boss."

"I'll remember you said that." His muscles tightened. "Are you ready?"

Laura braced her hands against the floor on either side of her. "Ready."

"I'm going to take it up slowly on three. One. Two. Three." He pressed, muscles screaming. The beam lifted an inch, then two. He focused on Laura's face, ready to stop in an instant if she showed signs of pain.

She pushed herself back smoothly, swinging her legs free of the beam. "I'm out." Her voice wobbled. "It's okay, I'm free."

He lowered the beam again cautiously and stumbled the few feet to her side. "Are you all right? Are you sure?"

All his professional detachment shattered into a million pieces at the need to hold her.

"I'm fine. Thanks to you." She turned into his arms, and he drew her close against him.

She was safe and in his arms where she belonged. *Thank You, Father. Thank You.*

He had no idea how much time passed before he felt

Laura stiffen. She pushed back away from him, her eyes wide with shock and fear.

"Smoke! I smell smoke—Ryan, we have to get out!"

"It's okay." He tried to hold her, but she'd pushed herself to her feet. "Honestly, it's all right. Everything's under control." He hadn't had the time or the brains to tell her what was happening in his fear for her safety.

She grabbed his arm and tried to pull him to the stairway. "We have to get out," she repeated, and he knew the memory of that other time was stark in her mind.

"It's all right." He put his arm around her and eased her toward the stairs. "We'll go down, but you have to be quiet. There's no need to hurry. I promise."

Laura wanted to grab Ryan and push him bodily down the stairs, but he was solid and immobile as a rock. The strength of his arm around her seemed to banish the panic that had erupted at the scent of smoke. Ryan knew what he was doing. She could trust him.

With his arm steady around her, they started down the stairs.

"Sure you're all right?"

She nodded, afraid to speak because her voice might betray the extent of her weakness. She felt as if she'd been hit by a bulldozer, but she'd be all right, thanks to Ryan. He'd rescued her yet again.

A few weeks ago she'd have angrily rejected the thought that she needed rescuing—or needed help of any kind. A few hours ago she'd still burned with the thought of Ryan's betrayal. The time she'd spent trapped and alone had changed everything.

She hadn't been alone. That was why. God had been with her. If was as if all her old fears had been wiped away in that short period. As if she were a new person, seeing through fresh eyes.

Her foot caught on a step, and she would have fallen if not for Ryan's arm around her.

"Shh." His voice was a bare whisper as they reached the bottom. "Stay right behind me and don't say a word."

She nodded, glancing at his face. Strong, intent, focused on something she didn't know about or understand. Holding her hand, he led the way toward the back of the house.

The smoky smell was stronger here, but musty, as if a blaze had been doused with water and still smoldered. He went softly across to the back door. Motioning for her to stay where she was, he edged the door open a crack.

She stepped closer to him, putting her hand on his back, feeling hard muscle and the warmth of his skin through the cotton of his shirt.

"What is it?" Her question was a mere breath, close to his ear.

"It's okay." He spoke in a normal tone, and he opened the door wide. "Looks like it's all over."

She blinked. The usually dark alley was alive with light. Red lights whirled on the top of a police car, painting the pavement in crimson stripes. The strong white beams of several flashlights bounced off brick and concrete.

A shiver went down her spine. Had they come to arrest her? "Ryan? What's happening?"

Several men clustered around something in the alley. One of them turned at the sound of her voice.

"Ms. McKay." Lieutenant North actually sounded welcoming. "Flanagan got to you, I see. Are you all right?"

"I'm fine," she said, wary of his sudden friendliness. "Why are you here?"

"Did we get him?" Ryan sounded impatient.

"Sure thing," North said. "We've got him all tied up in a neat package and ready to present to the district attorney's office."

"Get who?" Her voice shook a little.

"Didn't Flanagan tell you? We figured out who the arsonist was a few hours ago. And now he's been cooperative enough to walk right into our arms."

North took a step toward her, and she saw the person his body had shielded. The person who was handcuffed, slumped between two police officers. Bradley Potter.

The alleyway seemed to be spinning in time with the whirling red light. "I don't understand."

"No, I guess you wouldn't." North's voice gentled. "Mr. Potter does, however."

"I don't know what you're talking about." Potter's words were an octave higher than his usual smooth tones. "You're trying to frame me, and you won't get away with it. I demand to see my attorney."

He moved slightly, and one of the officers shifted his grip. His foot struck something that sloshed and rattled.

The beam of North's flashlight fastened on it. A can of paint thinner.

She could only stare at it, as conviction settled into her bones. Bradley Potter had tried to burn down her building. He'd attempted to finish the job tonight.

"Why would you do this? I don't understand. What do you have against me?" She took a step toward Potter, and Ryan grasped her arm.

"I don't think old Brad had anything against you, personally." The look Ryan turned on Potter was fierce enough to scald. "You and your renovation just threatened to sour the deal he had going."

"What deal? How could I possibly threaten him?"

"Brad put together a group to build a new hotel on this block. He already owned the surrounding buildings. This one was all he needed."

"But he could have just bought the building. Goodness knows I'm eager enough to sell. Why try to destroy it?"

"Because he couldn't buy it and tear it down. It's a protected historic building, remember? None of the surrounding buildings were, so he just bought them as they became available. I'd guess he was waiting for this place to be condemned, but you got in his way."

"Pure supposition." Fear showed beneath Potter's words. "You have no proof at all."

"We have eyewitnesses to arson." North nodded to the police officers. "Take him in."

She watched numbly as they put Potter in the back

of the police cruiser. It pulled out, swerving to avoid the paramedic van that turned into the alley.

"I still don't understand." Maybe her brain was fogged by too many traumatic events in too short a time. "Why——"

"Flanagan can explain it all to you later." North glanced from her to Ryan. "We owe solving this case to him. If he hadn't been so stubborn, you might be the subject of the charges we'll be making."

She searched Ryan's face. "Is that right? You did this?"

He shrugged, as if embarrassed. "Lieutenant North kept telling me to use my head. I guess I finally got the message."

He hadn't answered the question she'd really been asking, and maybe that was an answer in itself. Obviously, Ryan's new job was assured. He'd solved the case, and in the process he'd cleared her.

But he'd said nothing to indicate that he'd done it for any other reason. Nothing had changed between them, except that now she owed him her freedom.

"I—I have to get to the hospital." Mandy. She had to see Mandy.

North was already striding toward his car. "I'll meet you downtown, Flanagan."

Ryan squeezed her arm. "Sorry, but I have to go. The paramedics will take you to the hospital, and I'll stop by as soon as I can. All right?"

"You don't have to." She managed to smile. "Thank you, Ryan. For everything."

He nodded, already turning to go after North. He had

his job to do, and she couldn't delay him. And she also couldn't let him see that she wanted anything more from him.

She certainly looked as if she'd been dragged through a knothole backwards. Laura frowned at her reflection in the small mirror of the hospital bathroom. Circles under her eyes, a bruise on her temple, her hair a tangled mop—she'd had a rough night, and it showed.

She dragged a brush through her hair, trying to tame it. It didn't really matter how she looked. She wasn't going to be seeing anyone but Mandy, who didn't care as long as she was here.

Mandy had awakened happy this morning, apparently not bothered by the bruising and swelling on the side of her face that made Laura cringe in sympathy. If Mandy wasn't bothered by it, she couldn't show her reaction.

Deciding she wasn't going to look any better without a night's sleep, she went back into Mandy's room. Mandy looked up from the silent conversation she was apparently having with her old teddy, the stuffed puppy Nolie had brought, and the firefighter bear. She had lined them up against the bed's railing.

"Do you want anything else from your breakfast tray?" Laura signed.

Mandy wrinkled up her nose and shook her head. Laura found herself smiling.

"I don't blame you. When we go home later, you can have whatever you feel like eating."

She glanced at her watch. Dr. Phillips had said he'd

stop by later this morning, and if everything looked good, Mandy could go home.

Home. She didn't want to think about the mess on the third floor. How was she going to explain that? Maybe she ought to try and call Ms. Jamison and put her off.

I need some guidance, Father. It's my first day back to relying on You, and already I need help. Please show me how to handle this situation.

No immediate answer popped into her mind, but it didn't need to. The sense of peace she felt about it was enough to go on with.

Ryan hadn't come by, and she hadn't heard anything from him. That was all right, wasn't it? She'd made her peace with that, too.

Ryan wasn't ready for a family yet. He'd made his feelings clear. Someday he would be. She didn't doubt that even if he did.

But not yet. Not her and Mandy.

It's all right. Loving him has helped bring me back to You. I can't ask for more than that. I can't ask for something Ryan isn't willing to give.

The door swished, and Ryan walked in. Her heart gave a leap at the sight of him. She'd have to find a way of bringing that under control.

"Good morning." She studied his face. "You look almost as bad as I do. Didn't you get any sleep at all?"

He grinned. "Not so you could notice." He bent to kiss the top of Mandy's head. "Mandy's got her own black circles. We make quite a trio, don't we?"

Mandy smiled up at him, and Laura's heart gave another little jump. He was so good for Mandy. She'd blossomed since he'd come into their lives. If only—

No. I won't pick that up again, Father. I'll be content with whatever You have for us.

"Were you at headquarters all night?"

"Most of it." He shrugged, pulling a chair up and collapsing into it. "Then I went and had a little talk with your defaulting contractor."

"You did?" She hadn't given the man a thought since the previous night. "Why?"

"It occurred to me that Potter might have been behind his reluctance to do the job, along with some of the other troubles you had with people like the plasterers. So I thought it was worth a little talk."

She still couldn't quite get her mind around the fact of Potter's guilt. "Did the contractor admit it?"

"No, he wouldn't go that far. But oddly enough, the news that Bradley Potter was in jail completely changed his work schedule. His crew is at your place right now. By the time you get home, the third floor will look as good as new."

"That's wonderful." It was yet another thing she could hardly believe. And yet another thing she owed to Ryan. "Thank you. You've done so much for us that thanks don't seem enough."

His eyebrows lifted. "You're not mad at me for interfering?"

"No." The woman who'd used her independence as a weapon to keep people away was gone for good. "I'm just grateful. Not only did you rescue me, but you solved one of my biggest problems."

Ryan actually flushed. "It's nothing," he mumbled. "Anyway, that's not really why I came. I wanted to talk to you—"

"About the case, I suppose. How on earth did you get on to Potter, anyway?"

He blinked, as if he'd missed a step. "Oh, that. It sort of fell into our laps."

"That's not what North said. He said I owed it all to you."

"Actually to my stubbornness, I think he said. Funny, he was ready to fire me for that, but now I'm the golden boy of the arson squad."

She caught the message under his joking tone. "You risked your job to prove I didn't do it?"

He shrugged, as if embarrassed to admit it. "Well, I knew you hadn't done it. North wouldn't accept my instinct as proof, so I went back over the whole thing again. I think he wasn't really satisfied either, partly because of those anonymous calls we kept getting, as if someone was trying to lead us right to you."

Maybe it was better not to look too closely into Ryan's motives for risking his job. She didn't want to start hoping again.

"But how did you find out Potter was the one?"

He leaned back in the black vinyl chair. "I decided to interview the neighbors all over again, hoping someone had seen something. Nobody had, but someone did mention their landlord. Bradley Potter. And I remembered seeing him coming out of the building next to yours."

She remembered that day, too. "That surely wasn't enough to make you suspicious of him."

"It wasn't really what you'd call a suspicion—just an annoying little something that I wanted explained. When we looked, we found out he'd bought or had an option to buy all the buildings on that half block. Except yours." He shrugged. "Once we knew that, it wasn't hard to find out the rest."

"I still don't understand why he'd risk going to jail." A shudder went down her spine at the thought that it might have been her, if not for Ryan.

"Money. He wanted back what his father had lost, and he didn't care what he did to get it. He'd invested everything he had in this project, and without your property, he risked losing it all."

"He told you that?"

"No, he's still saying nothing without his lawyer. But I know." He moved restlessly in the chair. "I know what a guy will do to live up to his father's dreams."

"You found your own dream," she said quietly.

He shrugged. "Anyway, that wasn't what I wanted to talk to you about. I—"

The door swung open again. This time it was Siobhan and Brendan. Ryan glared at them.

"What are you doing here this early? I thought you were going to wait until later."

"Change in plans," Brendan said, his smile breaking through. "Nolie's in labor."

"She is?" Laura's heart leaped. "Is everything all right?"

"Just fine." Siobhan was reassuring. She hugged Mandy and handed her a glossy new book. "It'll be awhile, so we decided to come up and see how Mandy is doing."

"Mandy's doing fine." Ryan looked harassed. "I'm trying to talk to Laura, and I could do with a little less company."

Brendan pulled the door open, but he didn't go out. "I noticed the lounge is empty. You can go in there. We'll stay with Mandy."

"I don't—" Laura began.

Ryan interrupted her unceremoniously. He grabbed her hand and pulled her out of the chair.

"Come on." He tugged her toward the door. "Let's get out of here before any more of them show up."

Her heart was beating somewhere up in her throat as he pulled her across the hall and into the lounge. He shut the door firmly.

"I feel as if I should bar the door. Anything to get through this without being interrupted."

"Through what?" She managed to get the words out, but she couldn't kid herself that she sounded normal.

He crossed the space between them and took both her hands in his. The warmth of his touch robbed her of whatever breath she had left.

"I have to tell you this." His voice roughened and deepened on the words. "I saw pain in your eyes when you looked at me yesterday. It made me realize nothing was worth that—certainly not my job. It pushed me to do something I didn't think I had in me to do."

She couldn't have spoken if her life depended on it. She could only look at him, knowing he must be able to read her love for him.

"Thanks to you, I found out I didn't have to rely on sheer recklessness to rescue someone." He reached up to brush a strand of hair back from her face, and his fingers trembled against her skin. "When you called last night—when I saw you trapped and alone—" His voice broke.

She couldn't move. She couldn't speak. Seeing him let down all his defenses was enough to rip her heart open.

"Laura, I love you. I think I've loved you since the moment you came back into my life. I'm ready to stop running. I've found all I want in you and Mandy. Please tell me it's not too late."

She waited for all her doubts and her defensiveness to surface, keeping her from happiness. It didn't happen. She was free of them. Being right with God had made everything else in her life line up as well.

She reached up to stroke his cheek, loving the tenderness that shone in his eyes. "I was trapped by more than that beam until you came. Now—" The joy seemed to bubble up inside her. "Now I'm ready to share my life. I love you, Ryan Flanagan. Don't you dare walk out of my life again."

The joy dawned on Ryan's face. He drew her against him, his arms folding her close. "Never," he breathed against her hair. "Never."

Epilogue

Mandy sat on the high table in Dr. Phillips's office. Laura stood next to her, trying to keep any hint of apprehension from her face as they waited for the doctor to activate Mandy's implant. Ryan's hand pressed down on her shoulder, reassuring her, and she turned her head to smile at him.

The past month had gone by so swiftly it was hard to believe that so much in their lives had changed. Thanks to the quick work Ryan had ensured from the contractor, the building had been ready to show. The buyer had loved it and they'd closed quickly, enabling her to pay off the implant and have money left for a new start.

It was a start they'd made right here in Suffolk. Ryan would never want to move away from his family, and now that they were becoming her family and Mandy's family, she wouldn't part with them either.

Mandy touched her hand. I love you, Mommy.

"I love you, too, Mandy. I loved you before you were born, and I will always love you, whether you can hear or not." The words had become a ritual between them as they'd waited out the results of the implant.

"What about me?" Ryan signed. "You love me, don't you?"

Mandy's face crinkled in a smile. I love you, too. And baby Siobhan, and Grammy, and Grandpa, and my cousins and my puppy.

"At least I'm at the head of that list," he said, and dropped a kiss on her head.

Dr. Phillips stopped tinkering with the receiver. "I think we're ready," he said. "Let's give it a try." He switched it on and nodded at Laura.

"Mandy," she said, hardly daring to breathe.

Mandy's head jerked up instantly, her eyes wide with shock. Then a smile blossomed on her face, and she nodded.

Ryan's arms went around her, and his cheek was wet as he pressed it against hers. "She can hear. Our little girl can hear."

Thank You, Father. Her heart seemed to overflow with joy. *Thank You.*

* * * * *

Dear Reader,

I'm so glad you decided to pick up this book, and I hope my story touches your heart. The Flanagan firefighter series is very dear to me, and I hope you enjoy reading these books as much as I enjoyed writing them.

Ryan, the youngest of the Flanagan brothers, was quite a challenge to write about. A charmer like Ryan needed a very determined woman to show him that his future included marriage and family, and I found her in Laura, who had her own difficulties to face. I loved researching and writing about Laura's renovation project—maybe that's so appealing because it echoes our need to be made over in Christ's image.

I hope you'll write and let me know how you liked this story. Address your letter to me at Steeple Hill Books, 233 Broadway, Ste. 1001, New York, NY 10279, and I'll be happy to send you a signed bookplate or bookmark. You can visit me on the Web at www.martaperry.com or e-mail me at marta@martaperry.com.

Blessings,

Marta Perry

And now turn the page for
a sneak preview of

STORM CLOUDS
by Cheryl Wolverton,

part of Steeple Hill's exciting new line,
Love Inspired Suspense!

On sale in October 2005 from Steeple Hill Books.

Y*ou're coming, Angelina. You have no idea what you're walking into. I've waited a long time for this, and I'm not going to let you get in the way this time. Oh, no, not this time. I can kill two birds, as the saying goes. Angelina Harding. It's been a long time. And you're coming right to me here in Australia. You'll be within my grasp. Though this is going to put a kink in my plan, you're finally going to be mine. Time to play the mind games—again. And you won't even know it. Come on, Angie, doll. I'm waiting. Come on and try to find your brother and walk into the maze of my own making. Search for him and play awhile, before you die.*

The ride on the plane had been bumpy, with some of the worst turbulence Angelina Harding had ever experienced.

Oh, how she wanted to be back in Pride, Louisiana, the tiny little town with a population of less than one hundred. She'd lived there for three wonderful years now along with several of her friends who'd started a security firm. She liked it there in a small town, and didn't want to venture out into the real world.

But what could she do after she'd gotten the call— a call she hadn't expected? She hadn't talked to her brother in over fifteen years until last night. And he needed her help.

Stepping into the cool spring of Australia, she realized she had dressed not for spring but for late summer.

It was hot as a furnace in Baton Rouge.

And it was just finishing winter here.

She shivered and cupped her hand over her eyes to glance toward the sunny sky. Wearily she grabbed a handful of her dark hair, tied it in a knot at her neck and then released it when she realized it only made her feel cooler.

Her internal clock told her it should be nighttime.

Her brother had said to catch a plane to Sydney— and to hurry. Like she should drop everything for him. Glancing around, she noted the cars driving on the wrong side of the road.

She'd been so angry with her brother nearly twenty years ago when he'd become a Christian and decided to move to Australia....

She shook her head as she watched the hustle and bustle. Same as in any city, but different too.

What did they have in Australia? Not seeing her brother, she started down the sidewalk looking for any sign of him.

Okay, she knew Australia had wonderful beaches

and such, but then, she didn't like the fact her brother had moved to the other side of the world.

Bitterness nipped at her as she remembered her one previous visit to Australia. She'd been sixteen, and she'd come here to see her brother.

He had sent her back home after telling her she shouldn't have stolen money from their uncle, and she should have gotten his permission to come.

Permission!

She'd hated her brother for not letting her stay, and, yet, he was her brother, and when he'd called, she couldn't ignore him as he'd done to her.

Oh man, she didn't want to be here.

The beep of a horn as she stepped out in front of a taxi brought her back to the present. She back-pedaled.

She hated Australia.

Where was her brother?

"Angelina Harding?"

She heard her name called and turned in surprise.

A man of medium build with dark hair, dark trousers and a dark shirt stood about ten feet away. A small mole under his right eyebrow barely showed above the sunglasses he wore. In her job, she was used to cataloguing those she met. "That would be me," she acknowledged, noting he stood near a large sedan that already had a driver in it. She couldn't see much through the tinted windows, just that the car was unfamiliar to her.

"Your brother sent us."

Her eyebrows shot up and she glanced at the car

again. "He must be doing better than I realized," she muttered to the man, feeling even more angry and put out by her sibling. Swinging her backpack over her shoulder, because she refused to pack more than one small case when she traveled, she headed toward the car.

Her shoulders hurt, her neck ached. All she wanted to do was crawl in bed and sleep for a short while and try to adjust to the time change. "I can't believe it," she said as she climbed into the back seat. "He called me and demanded I show up here. Said he had to talk to me. Do you know what I dropped to be here?" She knew the man wasn't listening as he closed the door.

When someone says something like that, it *usually* means something serious is the matter, she thought, disgruntled. She'd been in the Secret Service. How could he simply stand her up like that? In frustration, she closed eyes and laid her head back on the seat. The soft leather cushioned her body and invited her to rest. When had Marcus been able to afford such a car? And why had he sent a car for her instead of picking her up himself?

As they drove, her mind drifted to her brother. All of those years ago when she'd last seen him, he'd lived in a tiny ranch house with no air conditioning, dusty, out in the middle of nowhere. A group of people had lived with him. Marcus had planned to start up a school in the area. He had even bought a van to pick the children up. He and his group were scraping by, but her brother had been so excited. This was his *calling*, he said.

Some calling, she thought sourly. Going out into the middle of nowhere to teach kids with accents.

There were plenty of kids in America with accents if that's what he liked.

She knew she was bitter, but she'd needed her brother, and he hadn't been there. However, *he* needed *her* now, and she was determined she'd be there for him. Regardless.

Angelina frowned and shifted in her seat when they hit a bump, realizing she'd dozed a bit. The smell of aftershave reached her nostrils, distracting her from her circle of thoughts, and she tried to place it. She couldn't remember the name, but she knew it was quite expensive.

Something niggled at her. Expensive car, expensive cologne. What was her brother into?

Cracking open her eyelid she glanced again at the two men in the front seats; neither had said a word. Suddenly, she noted something else. She'd been daydreaming longer than she'd realized, for they were outside of town. And the sun was on the wrong side of the car.

They were headed in the wrong direction.

Angelina might have only been here one other time, but she knew her directions and didn't forget something like that.

Alarm bells went off inside her. "Um, excuse me," she said to draw the attention of the man in the front seat. "How long before we get to where my brother is?"

The man shrugged. "Thirty minutes." Then a window between them slowly rose.

Now fully alert, she sat up. She did her best to keep her expression nonchalant as she glanced out the window because she saw the driver watching her closely. She nodded. "No problem. It's been many years. Just wondered."

Something wasn't right, and years of training told her that if she didn't get out of this car, she wasn't going to see her brother. Ever.

Love Inspired
SUSPENSE
RIVETING INSPIRATIONAL ROMANCE

Die Before Nightfall

BY SHIRLEE McCOY

A thirty-five-year-old mystery of tragic love becomes a very modern-day threat for nurse Raven Stevenson and her elderly charge's nephew Shane Montgomery.

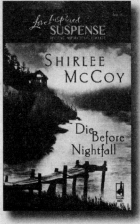

"A haunting tale of intrigue and twisted motives."
—Christy Award winner Hannah Alexander

Available at your favorite retail outlet.
Only from Steeple Hill Books!

Steeple
Hill®

www.SteepleHill.com

LISDBNSM

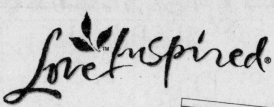

A SILENCE
IN THE HEART

BY

CAROLYNE
AARSEN

Vet technician Tracy Harris kept everyone at arm's
length—except one neglected neighborhood boy—
and veterinarian David Braun wanted to know why.
The more they worked together, the more he was
attracted to her. He longed to erase the sadness in her
eyes and help her reconcile with her past, so
she could move on to a future…with him.

Don't miss A SILENCE IN THE HEART
On sale September 2005

Available at your favorite retail outlet.

www.SteepleHill.com   LISIH

Take 2 inspirational love stories FREE!

PLUS get a FREE surprise gift!

Mail to Steeple Hill Reader Service™

In U.S.	**In Canada**
3010 Walden Ave.	P.O. Box 609
P.O. Box 1867	Fort Erie, Ontario
Buffalo, NY 14240-1867	L2A 5X3

YES! Please send me 2 free Love Inspired® novels and my free surprise gift. After receiving them, if I don't wish to receive anymore, I can return the shipping statement marked cancel. If I don't cancel, I will receive 4 brand-new novels every month, before they're available in stores! Bill me at the low price of $4.24 each in the U.S. and $4.74 each in Canada, plus 25¢ shipping and handling and applicable sales tax, if any*. That's the complete price and a savings of over 10% off the cover prices—quite a bargain! I understand that accepting the books and gift places me under no obligation ever to buy any books. I can always return a shipment and cancel at any time. Even if I never buy another book from Steeple Hill, the 2 free books and the surprise gift are mine to keep forever.

113 IDN DZ9M
313 IDN DZ9N

Name	(PLEASE PRINT)
Address	Apt. No.
City	State/Prov.	Zip/Postal Code

Not valid to current Love Inspired® subscribers.

Want to try two free books from another series?
Call 1-800-873-8635 or visit www.morefreebooks.com.

* Terms and prices are subject to change without notice. Sales tax applicable in New York. Canadian residents will be charged applicable provincial taxes and GST. All orders subject to approval. Offer limited to one per household.

® are registered trademarks owned and used by the trademark owner and or its licensee.

INTLI04R   ©2004 Steeple Hill

Suspicion
of Guilt

by Tracey V. Bateman

The Mahoney Sisters

Someone wants Denni Mahoney's home for troubled young women shut down, but could the threat be coming from inside?

"One of the most talented new storytellers
in Christian fiction."
—CBA bestselling author Karen Kingsbury

*Available at your favorite retail outlet.
Only from Steeple Hill Books!*

Steeple
Hill®

www.SteepleHill.com

LISSOGTVB

THE McKASLIN CLAN

ENJOY ANOTHER
McKASLIN CLAN STORY
WITH...

HEAVEN'S
TOUCH

BY

JILLIAN HART

After a combat accident, Special Forces soldier
Ben McKaslin returned home to recuperate, and ran
into his old friend Cadence Chapman. With his
career in tatters and his life on hold, he couldn't
allow himself to fall for her. But Cadence—and
God—had other plans for Ben....

The McKaslin Clan: Ensconced in a quaint mountain town
overlooking the vast Montana plains, the McKaslins rejoice
in the powerful bonds of faith, family...and forever love.

Don't miss HEAVEN'S TOUCH
On sale September 2005

Available at your favorite retail outlet.

www.SteepleHill.com   LIHTJH

Love Inspired

Tiny Blessings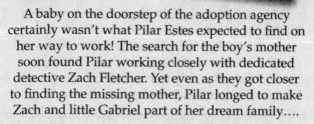

THE TINY BLESSINGS SERIES
CONTINUES WITH

ON THE DOORSTEP

BY

DANA CORBIT

A baby on the doorstep of the adoption agency certainly wasn't what Pilar Estes expected to find on her way to work! The search for the boy's mother soon found Pilar working closely with dedicated detective Zach Fletcher. Yet even as they got closer to finding the missing mother, Pilar longed to make Zach and little Gabriel part of her dream family....

Tiny Blessings: Giving thanks for the neediest of God's children, and the families who take them in!

**Don't miss ON THE DOORSTEP
On sale September 2005**

Available at your favorite retail outlet.

www.SteepleHill.com   LIOTD